MEET TH

Fortune of the ⟨...⟩

Age: 28

Vital statistics: The smart one *and* the pretty one. But don't waste your time.

Claim to fame: The last single Fortune Robinson daughter.

Romantic prospects: Her heart is shut up so tight it would take a crowbar to pry it open.

"After everything I've seen in my parents' marriage, I'd have to be crazy to want to get married myself. But I never intended to make my sister Sophie call off her own wedding! If I don't do something fast, she's going to lose Mason. He's one of the good guys. I can't let that happen.

Enter exhibit A: Alejandro Mendoza. Our family has a long-standing tradition of falling for Mendoza men, and Alejandro is the hottest hottie of the bunch. If I can make Sophie believe that I've fallen head over heels for him, her own cold feet will warm up. As for me? Having Alejandro as my make-believe boyfriend is a price I'm more than willing to pay. The trick is remembering it's just pretend..."

THE FORTUNES OF TEXAS: The Secret Fortunes: A new generation of heroes and heartbreakers!

Dear Reader,

How do you convince someone who has never been in love that love exists?

Olivia Fortune Robinson, my heroine in *Fortune's Surprise Engagement*, isn't a believer. She has a heart of gold and will go to the ends of the earth for the people she loves, especially her sisters. Olivia is always the bridesmaid until a family crisis has Olivia faking her own engagement to make her disillusioned sister believe that Olivia has had a change of heart. Who better to pose as Olivia's fake fiancé than Alejandro Mendoza? He's so tall, dark and drop-dead gorgeous that he has Olivia rethinking her hard-line stance on love in a heartbeat. There's something about Alejandro that's different from any guy she's ever met. Maybe it's because he's the one.

I hope you enjoy Alejandro and Olivia's story as much as I enjoyed writing it. Please look me up on Facebook at Facebook.com/nrobardsthompson or drop me a line at nrobardsthompson@yahoo.com.

Warmly,

Nancy

Fortune's Surprise Engagement

Nancy Robards Thompson

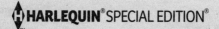
HARLEQUIN® SPECIAL EDITION®

Special thanks and acknowledgment to
Nancy Robards Thompson for her contribution to the
Fortunes of Texas: The Secret Fortunes continuity.

Recycling programs
for this product may
not exist in your area.

ISBN-13: 978-0-373-62347-1

Fortune's Surprise Engagement

Copyright © 2017 by Harlequin Books S.A.

Printed in U.S.A.

HARLEQUIN®

™ www.Harlequin.com

National bestselling author **Nancy Robards Thompson** holds a degree in journalism. She worked as a newspaper reporter until she realized reporting "just the facts" bored her silly. Now that she has much more content to report to her muse, Nancy loves writing women's fiction and romance full-time. Critics have deemed her work "funny, smart and observant." She resides in Florida with her husband and daughter. You can reach her at nancyrobardsthompson.com and Facebook.com/nancyrobardsthompsonbooks.

Books by Nancy Robards Thompson

Harlequin Special Edition

Celebration, TX

The Cowboy's Runaway Bride

Celebrations, Inc.

His Texas Christmas Bride
How to Marry a Doctor
A Celebration Christmas
Celebration's Baby
Celebration's Family
Celebration's Bride
Texas Christmas
Texas Magic
Texas Wedding

The Fortunes of Texas: All Fortune's Children

Fortune's Prince Charming

The Fortunes of Texas: Cowboy Country

My Fair Fortune

Visit the Author Profile page
at Harlequin.com for more titles.

This book is dedicated to Susan Litman and Marcia Book Adirim, the heart and soul of the Fortunes. And to Melanie Ashman for naming the signature drink Olivia served at Sophie's bachelorette party!

Chapter One

"It's time to break out the Fuzzy Handcuffs, Mike." Olivia Fortune Robinson gave the sexy bartender her most flirtatious smile.

He cocked a brow and grinned. "It's my pleasure to hook you ladies up."

"Excuse me?" Her sister Sophie frowned at him and then her eyes went wide as realization seemed to dawn. "Oh, no." Sophie held up her hands as if to ward off Mike. "Please tell me you are not a stripper." She pinned her panicked gaze on her sister. "Olivia, Dana and I specifically told you we didn't want strippers at our bachelorette party. No offense, Mike. I'm sure you're very good at what you do. You just can't do it here. Not tonight. Not for us."

She looked at her sister-in-law-to-be, Dana Trevino, and the other Fortune Robinson sisters seated on the plush love seats and overstuffed armchairs grouped around a glass cocktail table in a cozy corner of the Driskill Hotel bar.

Sophie's brown eyes were huge and color blazed high on her cheekbones. By contrast, Dana seemed to have gone pale as she perched hesitantly on the edge of her seat, as if weighing whether or not to bolt. Watching the pair of them squirm was worth all the effort Olivia had put into planning this sisters' weekend. Olivia almost hated to burst their horrified balloons.

"Unfortunately, Mike is not a stripper," she said, pausing to let them sit with thoughts of what they would be missing.

Her sister Rachel sighed. "Aw, that's too bad. For one glorious moment, I thought we had our very own Magic Mike."

Zoe, another sister, nodded in agreement.

Mike laughed. "Sorry, ladies. It's true, I'm not a stripper. Although I will be tending to your every need tonight."

The innuendo was thick.

"Does that mean you're a gigolo then?" Rachel asked, her eyes sparkling with mischief.

Mike laughed. "No, not a gigolo, either. I am your personal bartender and I am happy to be at your service."

Sophie's mouth formed a perfect O before her brows knit together. "And exactly what were you planning to do with the fuzzy handcuffs?"

Olivia and Mike exchanged a conspiratorial look.

"Forgive them," she said. "They don't get out much."

"There is nothing to forgive," he said. "Would you like to tell her about the Fuzzy Handcuffs or shall I?"

"Please, do the honors," Olivia said.

"Your sister commissioned me to create a signature cocktail for your bachelorette party." He stopped and looked at Sophie. "I'm guessing you are one of the brides."

"Yes, I'm Sophie."

He took her hand and lifted it to his lips before he asked, "Which one of you is Dana?"

"That would be me." The pretty redhead gave a hesitant wave before she tucked her hands into the fabric of her flowing gypsy skirt. Mike winked at her. Rachel and Zoe promptly introduced themselves, laughing as they made a dramatic show of extending their hands for a kiss. Mike didn't disappoint them.

Mike was a very good sport. As Olivia made a mental note to tell the manager how he'd gone above and beyond, her gaze was snared by a tall, dark, good-looking man walking into the bar. Though she only caught his profile before he turned and sat down with his back to her, he reminded her of someone. Who, she couldn't place, but Olivia hadn't gotten a very good look at him.

"Congratulations, ladies," Mike said. "I'm honored to serve you on your special night. I understand you're staying at the Driskill?"

"We are," Sophie said. "We checked in this afternoon. Olivia has planned a fabulous weekend for us."

"Nothing but the best for my sisters," Olivia said.

"When is the wedding?" he asked.

"Next weekend," Dana said. "Right here in this hotel in the ballroom. But there will be a full week of events leading up to the ceremony. This girls' get-together is a nice way to kick off the festivities."

"Well, don't let me hold up the party," Mike said. "One round of Fuzzy Handcuffs coming right up."

"Fuzzy Handcuffs." Rachel shook her head. "Only you would come up with a name like that, Olivia. Only you."

They all laughed.

"Originally, Mike wanted to call the drink the Bride's First Blush, but that was boring."

"No it's not," Sophie said. "It's pretty."

Olivia resisted the urge to roll her eyes. The name Bride's First Blush was too sweet for such a potent cocktail. The drink itself was perfect. It was festive and fizzy, but it also had just the right amount of something stronger to pack a pop. It needed a name that was just as strong, not one that sounded like a virgin cocktail. Fuzzy Handcuffs was perfect.

Olivia had gone to the ends of the earth to ensure that every single detail of this sisters' weekend was perfect. And of course, it had been perfect so far. She may have been a computer programmer by trade, but if she ever found herself in need of a career change, she did have a knack for event planning.

Sophie and Dana weren't party girls, so they'd

been ecstatic with the plan of a weekend of pampering. After they'd checked into the suite at the Driskill, a limousine had whisked them away to the spa where they'd enjoyed hot stone massages, facials, seaweed wraps, special conditioners that had brought out the shine in their tresses and luxurious aromatherapy soaks in jetted tubs. At noon, they'd taken a break from the pampering to enjoy a light lunch complete with mimosas. Afterward, they'd returned to the spa for mani-pedis before adjourning to the pool to sip fruit-infused reverse-osmosis water while they relaxed and soaked up just enough sun so not to burn, but to give them a healthy glow.

"I wanted my sister and sister-to-be's last weekend of freedom to be something you two will never forget. Since you nixed the strippers, I had to sneak in something edgy somewhere else. Voilà—Fuzzy Handcuffs. At least I didn't call it the Ol' Ball and Chain."

"No, that'll be the name of the drink we serve at your bachelorette party," Zoe quipped.

"Hell Froze Over might be a more apt name for my bridal cocktail, since that's what would happen if I ever got married."

"Don't be so cynical," Zoe said. "You reap what you sow."

"I beg your pardon?" Olivia knew exactly what her sister meant, but she wasn't going to give in that easily. Zoe was the consummate Pollyanna when it came to love and romance—despite every bad example their parents' screwed-up relationship and sham of a marriage had set for them.

"You know exactly what I mean." Zoe sighed and looked at Olivia as if she was hopeless. "You draw to you exactly what you put out into the world."

Olivia blanched, but now wasn't the time to get into a philosophical discussion about the realities of love and happily-ever-after. Besides the fact that this was supposed to be a happy occasion celebrating Sophie and Dana's imminent wedding, her other two sisters were newly married. Zoe was still in the honeymoon phase of her own marriage, having just wed Joaquin Mendoza last year. Rachel was married to Joaquin's brother Matteo.

Wait a minute—

Olivia's gaze found the tall guy at the bar. Was that the other Mendoza? The single one—what was his name?

She turned to her sisters. "See that guy over there? Isn't that your brother-in-law?"

They turned in unison and looked.

"Is that Alejandro?" Rachel said.

"I think it is," Zoe said.

"I didn't realize he was coming to town early," Sophie said. "We should say hi and invite him to join us for a drink." She started across the bar toward him and the next thing they knew, she was walking back arm-in-arm with him.

"Look who I found," Sophie said, triumphantly. "Alejandro, I'm sure you remember my sisters, Olivia,

Rachel and Zoe. And this is Dana, the other bride-
to-be."

They exchanged hellos.

"When did you get in?" Rachel asked.

"A couples of hours ago. I came in early to take
care of some business before the wedding."

All of the Mendoza men had been blessed by the
tall, dark and handsome Latin gene, but Alejandro
seemed to have gotten an extra helping of good looks.
Olivia wondered how she'd failed to notice that before
now. Of course, she'd only seen him on two other oc-
casions: Rachel's and Zoe's weddings. She'd brought
dates both times, so she hadn't exactly been looking.

"You came in from Miami, right?" Olivia asked.
She did remember that much.

He turned his sultry gaze on her.

"I did."

"I didn't realize you had business ties to Austin,"
Sophie asked. "What do you do, Alejandro?"

"I'm in the wine business," he said. "I'm a wine
sales rep, but I'm in town because I'm in the process
of buying a small vineyard about twenty miles west
of here."

Zoe's mouth fell open. "Your very own vineyard?
That's so cool. Why hasn't Joaquin mentioned it?"

Alejandro shrugged. "Until last week, it was still
up in the air, but everything finally fell into place.
I'm going to meet with the owners tomorrow and do
one last walk-through before we finalize the deal."

"Which winery?" Rachel asked.

"It's called Hummingbird Ridge." He kept stealing glances at Olivia.

"I've never known anyone who's actually owned a winery," Sophie mused. "I'd love to see it. Can you give us a tour?"

Alejandro's brows shot up as he considered the possibility. "I'm sure I can arrange a tasting for you. Is there time this week?"

Everyone looked at Olivia as if she was the keeper of the schedule. There were events and outings scheduled for every day of wedding week—tours of Austin for those from out of town, rounds of golf, tennis matches, couples' massages, luncheons, teas and dinners. But with a guest list close to five hundred people, the only activity they would all be doing as a group was watching the couples exchange their vows and celebrating at the reception afterward.

"How many people could you accommodate?" Olivia asked him.

"I'd say about two dozen," he told her. "Of course, I'll have to check with the winery and see how their availability looks. But this is their slow time of year when they don't get many large groups. It shouldn't be a problem. Maybe you can start organizing on your end and we can touch base and coordinate. Give me your number."

Out of the corner of her eye, Olivia saw Sophie elbow Zoe. The only reason she didn't make a face at them was because she didn't want to draw Alejandro's attention to their antics.

Olivia rattled off her cell number and Alejandro

put it in his phone, calling her to make sure he'd input the right digits. When her phone rang, Olivia entered his name.

"There," she said. "We should be all set."

Mike reappeared with a tray full of hot-pink cocktails. True to the drink's name, a pink-and-black fuzzy handcuff graced the stem of each frosted martini glass. A drink stirrer that seemed to be exploding silver tinsel decorated the top. The tray looked like a mini Fourth of July fireworks display.

As the five women expressed their delight, Mike looked pleased, but Alejandro took a step back.

"Why don't you join us for a drink, Alejandro?" Rachel said.

"Actually, he's welcome to mine," said Dana. "As much as I hate to leave this fabulous soiree, I have to go pick up my maid of honor from the airport. It's a pretty long haul out there. I really shouldn't drink and drive. I'm so eager to hug Monica. It's been ages. And she's bringing my wedding dress. She's letting me borrow an antique dress that belonged to her grandmother. I've seen pictures, but I haven't had a chance to try it on yet. I'm a little anxious about it. That's one of the reasons I need to go. I hope you understand."

Their future sister-in-law's early departure wasn't a surprise. Monica had made her reservations nearly simultaneously with Olivia finalizing the plans for the bachelorette party. While they wanted her to stay, they understood. Monica was like family to Dana, who had lost her parents in an accident when she was twelve and had grown up in foster care. While the guardianship had been adequate, it hadn't been warm enough to warrant keeping in touch or inviting them to the wedding.

The redhead, whose style was more boho-vintage than traditional, would look perfect in an antique gown. She twirled a long strand of copper hair around her index finger and drew in an audible breath.

"Wow. My maid of honor is arriving and I finally get to try on my dress. I guess that means this wedding is really happening." She put a hand on her heart. "I can't believe it's finally here."

The look of love was so evident in Dana's sparkling blue eyes that for the briefest moment, a pang of envy stabbed at Olivia's insides. It was an odd feeling. If given the chance, she wouldn't change places with her sisters. She cherished her independence. Even though the thought of tying herself to one man for the rest of her life made her feel claustrophobic, she was happy for her sisters. It was the happiness that she envied.

"I know." Sophie swooned. Feeling like an outsider, Olivia watched Rachel and Zoe coo right along with Dana and Sophie.

Her little sister, Sophie, and Mason Montgomery had gotten engaged in February, and just last month her brother, Kieran, had asked Dana to be his wife. Her siblings were certainly falling like flies bitten by the love bug. Olivia was the only one who hadn't succumbed. Even so, just because she didn't believe in the institution of marriage, it didn't mean she couldn't be happy for them.

That's precisely why she'd decided to go all out for Sophie and Dana's bachelorette party. Olivia couldn't resist a good party, especially when the guests of honor were women she adored and it gave her a chance to get together with her sisters Zoe and Rachel. Who, other than herself, could she trust to make sure that every detail was perfect?

"I'm so sorry you can't stay," said Sophie. "Why don't you pick up Monica and bring her back here? She could join us for dinner. As far as we're concerned, the more the merrier. Right?"

The sisters nodded. But Dana's left shoulder rose and fell. "As much as I'd love to, I can't. Monica is bound to be exhausted. But we will definitely come for brunch tomorrow, if that's still okay."

"We wouldn't have it any other way," Rachel said. "I'm sure you want a chance to catch up with Monica before everyone gets swept away by the festivities leading up to the wedding. It's going to be a busy week. And I know you want to try on your dress. I wish we could be there for that."

Sophie reached out and squeezed Dana's hand. "Of course, we completely understand. Monica needs to be rested up for the wedding. This really is the calm before the storm hits."

Something that sounded like a cross between a squeak and a squeal escaped from Sophie and she covered her mouth with both hands. She shook her head and wrung her jittery hands, excitement rolling off her in waves. "Oh, my gosh. You're right. It just got officially real. This time next week we will be married and dancing at our wedding reception. Maybe I should make my next Fuzzy Handcuffs a double."

"Good, that means you can have one for me," Dana said. "On that note, I'd better say good-night."

As the four Fortune Robinson sisters took turns hugging Dana, Alejandro, who had been silent since all the wedding talk started, spoke up. "I have some work to catch up on. I, too, will leave you ladies to your festivities."

His gaze caught Olivia's and lingered long enough to cause a slight shift in the room's temperature. It was like wading into a warmer current of water.

"Have fun," he said. "Olivia, I'll be in touch."

In reverent silence, the sisters watched Alejandro walk away.

"Gotta love those Mendoza genes," Rachel said under her breath.

"Oh, yeah. Highly recommended," Zoe said and sipped her drink. "Olivia, I think Alejandro is into you. You should go for him this week. Isn't it a lovely coincidence that he's Joaquin's last single brother and you're my last single sister?"

Sophie squealed. "I think Alejandro would be a perfect match for Olivia."

Olivia could think of many worse things than "going for" Alejandro Mendoza. A wedding fling with a gorgeous Latin man? *Hell, yeah.* It didn't get much better than that. Especially since he lived in Miami and she lived in Austin. That was just enough distance for a no-strings-attached fling.

A slow heat burned deep in her belly. She threw back her drink to cool herself off. The Fuzzy Handcuffs went down way too easily.

Yeah…but, no. Hooking up with Alejandro wasn't a good idea. He was family. Sort of. But not really. There was no blood relation. Her sisters were married to his brothers. That in itself was a problem. If she didn't handle the fling just right, it could get awkward at future family gatherings. And really, when was the last time she'd had a fling? Olivia liked to talk a good game, but she wasn't into casual sex. Anyway—

She plucked another drink from the tray and took a healthy sip.

"This night is not about me," she said. "It's about our sister and her happiness." She raised her glass high before she threw the drink back.

"Hear, hear," said Zoe. "I have an idea. Rather than a traditional toast, I think we should each take turns offering sweet Sophie our best words of sisterly advice for a long and happy marriage."

"Olivia, you go first," Zoe said.

Olivia frowned, already feeling the effects of the alcohol. "Marital advice is not exactly my department."

Zoe batted her words away. "Don't be a killjoy, Liv. You know what I mean. Give her your best sisterly advice."

Run! Run for your life. Get out now while you can still save yourself.

She chuckled at the thought. It was what she wanted to say, but even as tipsy as she was, she had enough good sense to know the reaction that comment would inspire in her sisters. Then she really would be the killjoy that Zoe had accused her of being. That wouldn't do. She'd have to dig deep to come up with something.

Of course, Zoe and Rachel and their husbands could be the poster couples for happy marriage. "You two go first. Come back to me."

As Rachel and Zoe spouted pearls of matrimonial wisdom, Olivia searched her soul to find something to offer—*anything*—that didn't sound jaded or bitter. But her head was spinning. Either she was a lightweight or these Fuzzy Handcuffs really did pack an über-potent punch.

That's when she realized three sets of sisterly eyes were focused on her, waiting expectantly.

"Guys, come on." Was she slurring her words? *Nah*, she was just thirsty. Water, she needed water. She looked over and signaled for Mike to come over. He gave her a thumbs-up, which Olivia took to mean he would be there as soon as he was free. He had a couple of customers at the bar, including Alejandro Mendoza. God, he was one sexy Texan—no, wait, he was from Miami. With a vineyard in Texas. So he was sort of an honorary Texy sexan…uhh, a *sexy Texan*. Whatever. He certainly was the best of both worlds: a head for business and a body for sin.

A body she really wouldn't mind taking for a test drive, she thought as she watched him sitting at the bar sipping his beer and doing something on his phone.

"Olivia!" Zoe demanded. "Earth to Olivia. We're waiting for you."

"Come on, Zo. You know I'm the worst person to ask about this. I don't believe in love."

She tried to wave them away, but realized that gesture probably looked as sloppy as she felt right now.

"How can you not believe in love?" Sophie pressed. Her voice went up an octave at the end of the sentence. "Everyone believes in love. I mean, what kind of a world would this be if people didn't believe in love?"

Rachel, who was still holding her first drink, shot Olivia a look. "You might want to slow down a bit, too. You're starting to be a bit of a buzzkill, Liv."

Oh, first she was a killjoy. Now she was a buzzkill?

"You want a buzzkill? I'll give you a buzzkill. I'm happy for the three of you, that you think you've found your soul mates. How fabulous for you. But just because it works for you, doesn't mean love and marriage are for me."

"It's because you're too guarded," Zoe said. "Of course you're not going to find love with that attitude. You have to open your heart before love can find you."

Rachel and Sophie nodded earnestly.

Olivia snorted. "Please tell me you're not going to start singing 'Kumbaya' in three-part harmony."

She rolled her eyes and when she did, she saw Alejandro looking in her direction. She looked away fast.

"I just don't understand why you feel that way," Sophie said in a small voice.

Olivia should've left it alone. She should've just made up something that sounded warm and fuzzy. Grabbed the first thing off the top of her head, something about love being the merging of two souls and blah, blah, blah, and tossed it at her sisters.

But they kept pressing her about *why*.

Why? Why? Why?

"You want to know *why* I don't believe in love? I'll tell you. Love is a crock. Every single guy I've dated has had some ulterior motive for dating me. They've wanted money or wanted a job or thought our father could make them rich by buying the app they've designed. They didn't want me as much as they wanted a piece of Robinson Enterprises."

"Sounds like you've been dating the wrong guys," Rachel said.

It was probably true, but there was something in Rachel's tone that sounded so judgmental. It was the last straw.

"And that's only half of it." Olivia leaned in and set her empty glass on the cocktail table. "The other reason is our parents. Their marriage is a mess. It's a phony sham of a relationship. I don't know why they stay together, because they hate each other. They are slowly but steadily eating each other alive. Anyone with good sense would take a clue from them and realize all relationships are doomed."

"But they're still together," Sophie said.

Olivia shrugged. "Why *are* they still together?

They don't love each other. Even if they did, what about the general state of society? Fifty percent of all marriages end in divorce and the other fifty percent—like our parents—make each other so miserable that divorce probably seems like a preferable option. And that's why I can see no reason to yearn for a doomed institution. On that note, why don't we go get something to eat?"

Her sisters sat stock still, silently staring at her. Rachel looked irritated. Zoe looked shell-shocked and Sophie looked like she was about to burst into tears.

Uh-oh. Obviously she'd gone too far.

"Look, you asked." She softened her tone. "That's why I didn't want to get into it."

All three were still frozen in their seats. The only thing that moved was the tears meandering down Sophie's cheeks.

Crap.

"Okay. I'm sorry. I understand that y'all are newlyweds—even you, Rach. So your relationships are still shiny and new—"

Now Sophie was shaking her head.

Sometimes it was as if she was the only one in her family who didn't have their head in the clouds. Maybe being the one with a clear head and common sense was her burden. If so, she could deal with it more easily than she could deal with a broken heart. She was a realist when it came to love—it never lasted. Her parents were living proof. Why should she fool herself into believing it would turn out otherwise for herself? Nope. She would save herself the heartache and focus on her career, which was in her control.

"I'm really sorry," Olivia said. "I didn't mean it the way it came out."

"Yes, you did." Sophie's voice broke and she stood up abruptly. "I'm tired and I want to go to bed."

"No, Soph. Come on. We need to get something to eat. I've made us a reservation at the Driskill Grill. I'm sure they can seat us early. Come on—"

"No." Sophie took off.

Her sister had barely cleared the bar when Zoe said, "I'll go check on her."

"I'll come with you," Olivia offered.

"No," Zoe and Rachel said in unison.

"Stay here," Zoe said.

"Bring her back," Olivia said. "It's Saturday night. It's her bachelorette party. We're supposed to have dinner. And then right after dinner, we're supposed to have fun."

"And clearly not a minute sooner," Rachel said under her breath, but Olivia heard her loud and clear.

"That wasn't very nice," she said.

Rachel shrugged. "Look, Olivia, I know you mean well, but why did you do that?"

"What?"

"Your down-with-marriage campaign was harsh. Even you have to admit it wasn't your best moment."

She covered her eyes with both palms. "I know. I already said I'm sorry. These Fuzzy Handcuffs are stronger than I realized. I think I'm a little drunk."

"Ya think?"

As if right on cue, Mike delivered another round of five Fuzzy Handcuffs.

"Who ordered these?" Olivia asked.

"I thought you wanted another round when you signaled me a few minutes ago."

"No, I need water."

"Oh, sorry," he said. "Well, these are on the house. I'll bring you some water."

Rachel stood.

"Where are you going?" Olivia asked.

"I'm going to go check on Sophie and Zoe."

"I'll go with you."

"No, stay here and drink some water."

"Will you please bring them back so we can go to dinner? I think we're all hungry. That's probably why the drinks hit us so hard."

Rachel sighed. "I'll try. I'll text you and let you know what Sophie is up for. Okay?"

As her sister walked away, Olivia sat down on the love seat. She'd already said too much tonight. The best thing she could do was give her sisters some space.

Fifteen minutes later, Rachel texted:

Sophie's asleep. Zoe is on the phone with Joaquin and frankly, I'm exhausted. I think it would be best if we call it a night and start fresh with the brunch tomorrow morning.

I'm sorry I ruined the night. I feel so bad.

Not your fault. I think the reality of the wedding is finally hitting Sophie. She'll be fine tomorrow.

Olivia wasn't mad; she was frustrated. This wasn't the way tonight was supposed to turn out—her sister in tears and the evening going up in flames.

Okay, maybe she was a little bit irritated. Why had they pushed her? Why had she been so weak as to give in? Sophie'd get over it. They'd be fine, but she needed to stay away until they all cooled off.

Olivia texted her again:

I'll be up after I get something to eat. Want me to bring you something?

Thanks, but no. I'm going to talk to Matteo and then I'll call it a night. Are you okay? Do you just want to come up to the suite and order room service?

It dawned on Olivia that her married sisters missed their husbands. Melancholy pushed at Olivia's heart. As she looked up from her phone, thinking about how to answer, she caught Alejandro Mendoza looking at her. This time she didn't look away.

She had plenty of drinks in front of her and a reservation for dinner for four that was about to become dinner for two. Olivia texted: I'm fine.

And she was about to get a whole lot better.

Alejandro couldn't hear what the Fortune Robinson sisters were talking about on the other side of the bar, but one minute they'd been toasting, raising their Fuzzy Handcuffs high, and the next it looked like they were arguing.

He shouldn't have been watching them. They were out for a girls' night, which appeared innocent enough, but what man in his right mind could've kept his eyes off such a collection of beauties? They were like magnets. He couldn't help but steal glances their way. His brothers were lucky men. Sophie would soon be married. What about Olivia? No doubt he'd meet the fortunate dude who'd claimed her heart at the wedding.

They'd seemed oblivious to him even as one by one they'd gotten up and left the party. First, Sophie left looking upset, followed by Zoe looking concerned. And finally Rachel, looking like a mother hen.

Olivia was the only one who remained. She'd been sitting alone for a solid five minutes staring at the tray of drinks the bartender had delivered shortly before the mass exodus. Maybe her sisters were coming back? Maybe she could use some company until they did. Alejandro stood, slid his phone into his shirt pocket and went over to Olivia.

"Is the party over already?" he asked.

She blinked up at him as if he'd startled her out of deep thought—or deep, stubborn brooding, based on her irritated expression. That full bottom lip of hers stuck out a little more than he remembered from when he saw her at his brothers' weddings.

As she gazed up at him, she pulled it between her teeth for a pensive moment before she spoke.

"May I ask you a question, Alejandro?" She slurred her words ever so slightly.

"Sure."

"Do you believe in love?"

"Is that a trick question?" He laughed and cocked his right brow in a way that always seemed to get him out of tight spots and trick questions like this one.

Answering questions about love qualified as a very tight spot, because the last thing he wanted to do right now was get into a debate about affairs of the heart with a woman who'd had too many Fuzzy Handcuffs. In his experience, drunk women pondering love were usually vulnerable women, especially when their sisters were all married or in the process of getting hitched.

"No, it's not a trick question," Olivia said. "In fact, it's a fairly straightforward yes-or-no query. You either believe in love or you don't. So what's it going to be, Alejandro? Yes or no?"

Wow. Olivia Fortune Robinson was a force. An intense force. And he could see that she wasn't going to let him off the hook without a satisfactory answer. The problem was, he didn't want to talk about love.

He'd been a believer once—but that was a long time ago. Another lifetime ago, when things were a lot simpler. So simple, in fact, that he'd never had to ponder love's existence. He'd just had to feel; he'd simply had to *be*.

He hadn't thought about love for a very long time.

It had been even longer since he'd felt any emotion even remotely resembling it. In fact, these days he didn't feel anything. But he definitely didn't want to conjure ghosts from the past, because they haunted him randomly even without an invitation.

"You're not going to answer me, are you?" Olivia said.

He smiled to lighten the mood. "That's some heavy pondering for such a festive occasion. Where did everybody go? And more important, are you going to drink all those Fuzzy Handcuffs all by yourself? Because if your sisters left you to your own devices, what kind of gentleman would I be to let you drink alone?"

She gestured with an unsteady wave of her hand.

"Don't worry about me. I'm used to drinking alone." She grimaced. "And even though I might be a little tipsy, I'm not so drunk that I don't realize how pathetic that just sounded. Please, sit down and save me from myself."

"If you insist," he said and lowered himself onto the cowhide-patterned love seat that was set perpendicular to her chair. As he made himself comfortable, she shifted her body so that she was angled in his direction and crossed one long, lean, tanned leg over the other.

Damn.

If he'd been a weaker man he might have reached out and run a hand up the tempting expanse, past where skin disappeared under that sexy little black slip of a thing that was riding a little too high on her toned thighs—not in a trashy way, because there wasn't a trashy thing about her. Olivia Fortune Robinson seemed to have mastered the art of classy-sexy, which was a very beautiful fine line to walk.

And he was also treading a very fine line, because Olivia Fortune Robinson was so very off-limits, since she was practically family.

He lifted a drink off the tray and handed it to her, then he took one for himself and raised it to hers. She looked him square in the eyes as they clinked glasses.

"You know, they say you'll have seven years of bad sex if you don't look the person you're toasting in the eyes as you say cheers," she said.

"I guess that means we'll have good sex," he said, still holding her gaze.

"Will we?" She sipped her drink.

He knew she was baiting him and he also knew she was probably drunker than she realized. The drinks were more powerful than they looked. The kind that went down easily and, before you knew it, knocked you flat on your ass. Probably not so dissimilar from the effect that Olivia Fortune Robinson had on men.

"Are you hungry?" Olivia asked.

"For food? Or did you have something else in mind?"

She tilted her head to the side. "You're a naughty boy, aren't you, Alejandro?"

Her words were unwavering and unabashed.

He shrugged.

"I made a dinner reservation for four at the Driskill Grill," she said. "It seems my sisters can't make it.

The only thing worse than drinking alone is dining alone in a fancy restaurant. What do you say, Alejandro? Will you let me take you to dinner?"

"That depends on what you expect in return," he said. "Are you going to feed me and then try to take advantage of me?"

"Absolutely."

This was fun. Much more fun than poring over facts and figures of the Hummingbird Ridge purchase.

When he was fresh out of college, would he have found bantering with a clever woman preferable to dotting the *i*'s and crossing the *t*'s on the details that would make his hard-won business dream a reality? Then again, he hadn't eaten and he was starving.

"In that case," he said, "how can I refuse?"

He knocked back the last of his drink. It was a lot stronger that it appeared.

"Good," Olivia said, handing him another drink from the tray. "The reservation isn't until eight o'clock. We have time to finish our cocktails."

They clinked glasses, locking gazes again before they sipped and settled into an uncomfortable silence. Alejandro was way too aware of how damn sexy she looked in that black dress, too intent on that full mouth that kept commanding his attention, speaking to the most primal needs in him.

He didn't do well with silence.

"Is this your favorite kind of drink?" he asked.

"Me? No. I'm all about champagne. This drink was made especially for the brides-to-be."

"I don't mean to be nosy, but is everything okay with your sisters?"

She shrugged. "I'm sure they're fine. That reminds me. You didn't answer my question. Do you believe in love? I'm guessing you do. Because what else would possess you to tattoo a woman's name on your arm? Who is Anna?"

Reflexively, his right hand found his left forearm, covered the ornate script.

"Anna was someone who made me know that love is very real. But I also learned that love can be a total SOB, too."

Olivia leaned in. "You said 'was.' So I'm guessing that Anna is no longer in the picture?"

The curtain of dread that always closed around him when he remembered Anna started falling. "No, she is no longer in the picture."

That's all he was going to say. He was opening his mouth to change the subject when Olivia got up from her chair and sat down next to him on the love seat.

"That's what I was hoping you'd say," she slurred. "People accuse me of a lot of things, but no one can ever say I go after another woman's man. You don't have a girlfriend who isn't named Anna, do you, Alejandro?"

He shook his head. His gaze fell to her lips. She was sitting enticingly close to him. Suddenly, the room temperature seemed to spike.

"Good," she slurred again as she slid her arms around his neck. "Because I'm going to kiss you. You don't mind if I kiss you, do you, Alejandro?"

Before the words *hell no* could pass his lips, her lips closed over his and smothered the reply.

At first, the kiss was surprisingly gentle, tentative. She tasted like the cocktails they'd been drinking and fresh summer berries and something else he hadn't realized he'd been craving for a very long time. When she opened her mouth wider, inviting him in, passion took over and the gentle kiss morphed into wild, ravenous need, feeding a hunger that he didn't realize was consuming him. He reveled in it, wallowed in it, until it blocked out everything else.

She moved against him, sliding her hands over his shoulders and down his back.

A rush of hot need surged through him. His hands followed the outline of her curves until he cupped her bottom and pulled her closer. Damn. She felt good. Keeping one hand on her, he found the hem of her dress with his other and dipped his fingertips beneath the silky barrier that stood between them.

When she moaned into their kiss, he wanted to pull her onto his lap.

But she was drunk and they were in the bar of the hotel where her sister was getting married next weekend. He had enough of his wits about him to know that if she wasn't in the shackles of too many Fuzzy Handcuffs, she probably wouldn't be doing this. She'd probably be mortified tomorrow.

"Alejandro, take me to your room." Her words were hot on his neck and his body was saying *Let's go. Now.*

But he couldn't. And not for lack of want or interest. It just wasn't right. Not when she was like this.

He stood up and gently tugged her to her feet. "What's your room number?"

Chapter Two

"Olivia, wake up."

The soft voice bounced around her dreams, beckoning her to open her eyes. Maybe if she ignored it, it would go away and she could go back to the dream of kissing Alejandro... His hands in her hair, pulling her mouth to his; him slowly but firmly guiding her in a backward walk, until he'd pinned her against the wall... His fingers lacing through hers, then pushing their joined hands out and up over her head so she could feel the length of his body pressed into hers.

It was glorious and she wanted more of him, all of him.

"Olivia. I'm not kidding. Wake up. It's an emergency." Why was Rachel's voice in her dream? She was intruding again. Only this time she was being more insistent and it seemed like she wasn't going away. Olivia tried to force her eyes open...to no avail.

"Olivia." Something was shaking her body in a way that didn't mesh with Alejandro's tender caresses. She managed to force one eye open. She saw Rachel's and Zoe's anxious faces staring down at her as searing pain shot through her head.

She felt as if someone had clocked her.

As she pressed the palms of her hands over her eyes, everything came back to her. She'd been clubbed by one too many Fuzzy Handcuffs. Okay, maybe a few too many. And then there was Alejandro. She'd all but had him for dinner. Kissing him hadn't been simply a dream. It had been very real—

Oh, no.

"Olivia, wake up!" It was Rachel shaking her. "We have a situation."

At the sound of her sister's no-nonsense tone, Olivia removed her palms from her eyes and forced her eyes open. For the love of God, her head was about to split wide open.

"It's Sophie," Zoe said. "She's missing. We can't find her anywhere."

It took a moment for Olivia to piece together last night's events: the drinks, her spilling the beans to her sisters about how she felt about their parents' relationship—or lack thereof—Sophie getting upset and running off.

"What do you mean she's missing?" Olivia asked. "Maybe she went out for coffee?"

Every word was a nail in her brain. Her mouth

was so dry her lips stuck to her gums like they'd been pasted together. She needed water. It probably wouldn't be a good idea to ask them if they could go look for Sophie and bring her back a bottle of ice-cold water.

"Do you think she's in danger?" Olivia asked.

Rachel and Zoe looked at each other.

"No," Rachel said. "Otherwise we would've called the police."

"All of her stuff is gone," Zoe said. "She must have packed up and taken it with her. And I must've been sleeping deeply because I didn't even hear her moving around."

Zoe and Sophie had shared one room in the two-bedroom suite. Olivia and Rachel had shared the other one.

"Personally, I think she's freaked out over what you said last night and has cold feet," Zoe said. "You know, prewedding jitters. I get it. I totally understand. It happened to me. That's why we need to find her and let her know the way she's feeling is perfectly normal and everything will be all right."

"Have you talked to Mason?" Olivia's voice was scratchy. "I'll bet she's with him."

Again, Rachel and Zoe exchanged a look.

"He just called. In fact, his call woke Zoe up," Rachel said. "He was looking for Sophie."

"Did you tell him she's at her bachelorette party and that means no boys? He can live without her for a weekend."

Zoe sighed. "Normally, I would've told him that,

but he said she'd left him a distraught message last night after he'd gone to bed. Apparently she said she needed to talk to him as soon as possible and he should call no matter the hour. Now she's not picking up, and she hasn't returned any of his calls or mine. We're worried about her, Liv."

Olivia regarded her sisters, who were still in their pajamas. "I'm guessing you haven't gone out to see if she's down in the café? She might've just gone out for some breakfast or some fresh air."

Olivia could have used both right about now.

She forced herself into a sitting position, trying to ignore the daggers that stabbed at her brain and filled it with a soup-like fog that refused to let her think straight.

As if reading her mind, Rachel produced a bottle of cold water and a wet washcloth.

"You look like hell," she said. "You're positively green. Drink this and wipe your face with this cool cloth."

Olivia did as she was told. Only then did she realize she was still fully dressed in the outfit she'd worn last night. At least she was dressed. She might have smirked at the thought, if the reaction wouldn't have hurt so badly. Of course she was dressed. She'd only kissed Alejandro. She hadn't slept with him. The memory of him walking her up to the suite and the two of them indulging in a delicious good-night kiss right outside the door flooded back. Her sisters didn't need to know about that. Besides, they had more important things to worry about with Sophie going AWOL.

"What time did you get in last night?" Zoe asked.

Olivia took a long drink from the water bottle. When she was finished, she said, "I don't know. Late. You all jumped ship and left me with a tray full of drinks to polish off. It took a while."

Zoe frowned. "I'm sorry we left. We were concerned about Sophie after your little down-with-love tirade."

Tirade?

It hadn't exactly been a tirade. It'd been honesty.

"Yeah, well, I wish you wouldn't have kept pushing me to offer love and marriage advice. I felt like you backed me into a corner."

The sisters sat in silence for a moment.

"Of course, the drinks didn't help matters," Olivia said. "They sort of greased the hinges on propriety's trapdoor and once the words started spilling out, there was no stopping them. I feel bad that Sophie was so upset. It wasn't what I intended."

The washcloth had warmed up. Olivia held it by the corners and waved it back and forth to cool it off before pressing it pressed to her eyes again.

Visions of kissing Alejandro played out on the screen in her mind's eye. She was so glad her sisters hadn't pressed her about whether or not she'd polished off the remaining drinks alone. The thought of those Fuzzy Handcuffs made her stomach churn, and the thought of trying to explain what happened with Alejandro tied it up in knots.

Olivia looked at her sisters. "Was Sophie here when you went to sleep?"

"She was," said Zoe.

"In fact, I thought she was out like a light when I finally turned in. I tried to talk to her before she went to bed, but she said she was fine and just wanted to go to sleep. So I went in and took a shower and then I was on the phone with Joaquin for a while. When I came out of the bathroom, she was snuggled down under the covers. I thought she was just missing Mason."

"Me, too," said Rachel. "But that's why we're concerned that he can't get in touch with her. Where do you think she would go?"

"So obviously you two haven't even been out of the room," Olivia said.

"No, not yet," Zoe said. "We hated to wake you since you obviously played a little hard last night." She gestured to Olivia's outfit.

"Not really. It's not as if I did the walk of shame this morning."

But she had kissed Alejandro. The thought made her already knotted, churning stomach clench a little bit more. She put her hand on her belly to quell it.

It would've been easy to give in to lust and do a lot more than kiss Alejandro last night, but she hadn't. Actually, she'd tried, but he'd been the gentleman.

Even so, the essence of him clung to her. Like he had gotten into her pores. If she shut her eyes, there was Alejandro invading her thoughts the same way he had invaded her dreams. Her fingers found their way to her lips as she remembered every delicious detail about their kisses.

Olivia had a lot of faults, but getting blackout drunk wasn't one of them. No matter how much she had to drink, she was always in control of herself. Sometimes it made her a little looser. She paused. Maybe *looser* wasn't the best word in this particular situation. The Fuzzy Handcuffs had unshackled her inhibitions. That was a more apt description. The drinks had simply allowed her to experience a pleasure in which she might not have otherwise allowed herself to indulge. Yes. That was what'd happened.

She was more than willing to own her actions.

And in owning them, she had enough good sense to know kissing Alejandro last night was as far as things would go. She'd gotten him out of her system and it wouldn't happen again. Of course not. She would be far too busy focusing on her bridesmaid's duties this wedding week.

As fractured as the night had been with her sisters, it was still a girls' weekend. Never mind how gorgeous Alejandro Mendoza was. She'd resisted him. She hadn't bailed on her sisters to spend the night with him.

Even if her sisters had bailed on her.

With great care, Olivia swung her legs over the side of the bed. She put her feet flat on the floor, hoping that the effort would ground her and help her regain her sense of equilibrium. Instead, the room spun. She hated being hungover, but she'd done this to herself. She had no choice but to power through. Do the crime, do the time.

"You do look like hell," Zoe said.

"I'm fine," Olivia answered, pushing to her feet.

"I'm going to get dressed and head downstairs to look for her," Rachel said. "Will you help me look, Liv? I think Zoe should wait in the room in case she returns."

She considered asking, *What if she doesn't want to be found right now? What if she just needs a little time? I'm the one who has a pounding headache. Why can't I wait in the room?* But she knew this was their way of nudging her to make amends with Sophie. To go look for her and find her so the two of them could talk this out and make up.

Of course, that's what she intended to do. She took a deep breath and tried to shake off the irritation that prickled her. How had this suddenly become her fault?

Olivia knew her sisters meant well. This was simply their sister dynamics in play: Zoe was the hopeful one; Rachel was the strong one; Sophie was the baby; Olivia was the one who fixed problems and rallied everyone to take action.

Often, Rachel and Zoe formulated a plan and Olivia made sure it got done.

Olivia cleared her throat and shook off the cobwebs from last night the best she could. It gave her a little more clarity. She made a mental note to have someone kick her if she ever felt compelled to finish off a tray of drinks. Though it would surely be a while before she imbibed again.

Her sisters were chattering at her. As their words bounced off her ears, she pulled jeans, a black blouse and fresh undergarments out of her suitcase and disappeared into the bathroom.

"I have to take a shower before I do anything," she said.

"We can go down to the lobby together," Rachel said. "I'll talk to the bellhops and ask if she called for a cab or if they remember her taking an Uber. Since we all rode here together, we know she didn't drive away and I doubt she walked. We can split up and have a look around the hotel."

Minutes later, after they'd dressed, Olivia grabbed her cell phone and room key and said to Zoe, "Let us know if you hear from her and we'll do the same."

When they got down to the lobby, Olivia looked around as if she might see Sophie standing there waiting for her. She wasn't there, of course. Next, they pulled up a picture of Sophie that Olivia had taken last night with her cell phone and asked the attendants at the porte cochere if they'd called a cab for her or seen her this morning. They hadn't. Next they decided to split up and each search a different half of the hotel.

Had Sophie really taken her words to heart? Regret churned in Olivia's stomach, adding to last night's bile, making her feel sick again. Only this time it had less to do with the Fuzzy Handcuffs and more to do with her big unfiltered mouth and how it had shoved her sister down this spiral of doubt on the eve of wedding-week festivities.

She had to fix this. She would fix this.

She decided to check the café first since it seemed a likely place to find Sophie.

Olivia pulled open the beveled glass doors of the 1886 Café & Bakery and stepped inside. The place was buzzing with families and couples and individuals sitting at the dark wooden tables and booths enjoying Sunday breakfast. She scanned the room with its white honeycomb tile floor and kelly green accent wall that separated the open kitchen from the dining room, and the flagstone archways that partitioned the dining room into smaller, more intimate sections. She fully expected to see Sophie sitting at one of the tables, noshing on a warm chocolate croissant and a café latte.

The place was crowded so Olivia had to walk around. As she did, she breathed in delicious breakfast aromas. Maybe, she thought, a good breakfast would be the cure for her hangover. Or at least the start. But first—Sophie. She would locate her sister—it couldn't be that difficult, even though she clearly wasn't in the café—and then she would treat herself to something delicious. In fact, it would be a good idea to treat Sophie to breakfast too, so they could talk things out and settle this once and for all.

Speaking of delicious…

As if she'd conjured him, there sat Alejandro Mendoza, at a small table tucked into a corner of the restaurant. He was enjoying a hearty omelet that looked like it could feed three people. As if he sensed her watching him, he looked up from the piece of the Sunday *New York Times* that he had folded neatly into quarters, allowing him to read while he dined. He snared her with his gaze before she could turn away and pretend she hadn't seen him.

That sexy, lopsided smile of his that crinkled his coffee-colored eyes at the corners made her breath catch. Visions of kissing him last night—of how perfectly their mouths and bodies had fit together— flooded back, swamping her senses and throwing off her equilibrium.

Get it together, girl.

"Good morning," she said, trying her best to appear nonchalant, to act as if it hadn't taken every fiber of her willpower to go to bed alone last night rather than give in to the chemistry that pulsed between them. She could still feel his kisses on her lips. Her mouth went dry at the thought and she bit her bottom lip to make the memory go away. As if.

He looked her up and down and smiled as if he approved of what he saw. She was acutely aware of the fact that her face was scrubbed fresh and makeup free. She'd pulled her long dark wet hair into a simple ponytail. She felt exposed and vulnerable, but he didn't seem to be turned off by her appearance. Not that it mattered. In fact, maybe it would be better if he was turned off because she would want nothing to do with someone that shallow. Still, she sensed that Alejandro Mendoza might be something of a player.

Maybe he was playing her right now.

"Good morning," he said as he stood. "You're up early."

"So are you," she returned.

He laughed, a deep sound that resonated in her soul and wove its way through her insides.

"Please sit down and enjoy your breakfast," Olivia said. "I don't want it to get cold."

He waved her off and remained standing.

"I have to drive over to Hummingbird Ridge for a business meeting later this morning," he said. "I wanted to grab a bite before I go. Join me. You know what they say about breakfast. It's the most important meal of the day."

The thought of having breakfast with Alejandro conjured all kinds of other possibilities—of what might have happened after the kiss and before the eggs and bacon if she hadn't said good-night—but Olivia blinked away the naughty thoughts.

"Thanks, but I'm looking for Sophie. You haven't seen her, have you?"

He looked confused. "Not since last night before she left the bar."

"So she hasn't been here this morning?"

"Nope. Please join me until she comes." He pulled out the other chair at the table for two.

Needing an ear, she sat down and he helped her scoot in her seat, and he motioned for the server to bring another cup of coffee.

She appreciated his gentlemanly way. Of course, she was perfectly capable of scooting in her own chair, but she had to admit the gesture was nice. It said a lot about him. She thought that chivalry had become a dying art these days. It was nice to meet someone with such good manners.

She bit her bottom lip again as she weighed how much to tell him. He already knew that Sophie had left last night's party upset and that Olivia's blunt words about love had offended her. They'd kissed and shared that secret. She might as well share this, too.

"I can trust you, right?"

He leaned in and studied her, as if he was trying to figure out what she meant, but he nodded. "Of course."

The server delivered a cup of coffee. After adding cream, she took a sip and felt some of the fog lift from her brain. She leaned in and rested her chin on her left hand, toying with the handle of the mug with her right.

"When my sisters and I woke up this morning, Sophie was gone."

"Gone? As in…?"

"Gone. As in packed up her things and left."

"She's not in any danger, is she?"

"We don't think so. Well, not physical danger, anyway. Maybe in danger of calling off the wedding because of my unfiltered tirade on love. I need to find her and fix this."

Alejandro looked concerned. "Have you called her fiancé?"

"He called us, saying he couldn't get in touch with her. That she'd called him last night while he was sleeping and left a couple of messages, and when he tried to call her this morning he couldn't reach her. She wasn't picking up. I've looked all over the hotel and she's not here. The best I can figure is that she called an Uber and left."

"Where would she go?"

Olivia thought for a moment, changing gears from likely hiding places in the hotel to where Sophie might go outside of the place. She had an idea.

"We know she's not at Mason's. He said he'd call if he heard from her. I can think of a couple of places I'd look to start. She probably went home to her condo."

She shook her head. "I'm going to have a lot of explaining to do when I find her."

"Don't jump to conclusions," Alejandro said. "Maybe it's not as bad as you think."

Olivia shrugged. "My sisters and I think that last night sent her spiraling into a case of prewedding jitters. You know, cold feet."

Alejandro opened his mouth as if to say something, but sighed instead.

"What?" Olivia asked.

"Nothing."

"No, it's something. Tell me, please."

"If she's so easily spooked, maybe she knows something we don't."

"Such as?"

"Maybe she's questioning whether she should get married or not. If so, that's not your fault. In fact, maybe you did her a favor. Maybe what you said made her think. If she's having second thoughts, isn't it better to call off the wedding than to get a divorce?"

"We can't call off the wedding, because it's Dana and Kieran's wedding, too. And if Sophie opts out, it will certainly put a damper on their day."

"So you're saying truth be damned? She should just suck it up for propriety's sake? Because if so, maybe you're not as antiestablishment as you think you are."

She squinted at him. "That is *not* what I'm saying. This has nothing to do with me and everything to do with my sister's happiness."

"But you're making it sound like this is all about you. You must think you have some kind of power over her if you think your feelings about love and marriage can change her mind."

"I'm not saying I changed her mind. I'm saying I've spoiled the mood, cast a black cloud and now she's got cold feet."

Cocking a brow that seemed to say he wasn't convinced, Alejandro sat back and crossed his arms. He looked at her as if the judge and jury resided inside his head and they'd already come to a verdict on the matter. "You're saying all you have to do is talk to her and you can change her mind."

It wasn't a question. It was a statement, and Olivia didn't like the implications. She stood.

"Look, you don't know me or my sister. I don't know why it seemed like a good idea to burden you with the details. So please forget everything I told you. Sophie will be fine. The wedding will be fine. Good luck with your meeting."

As she turned to walk away, something made her

turn back. He watched her as she returned to the table. "I hope it goes without saying, but please don't mention this to anyone. Okay?"

"Of course. And I won't mention the kiss, either."

He had the audacity to wink at her. All cheeky and smug-like. That's what he was—cheeky and smug. And a player who took advantage of drunk women.

Okay, so maybe the kiss wasn't so bad.

Olivia flinched and waved him off. Her stomach remained in knots even as she made her way into the majestic Driskill's lobby, away from Alejandro Mendoza. The guy was a piece of work. A smug, cheeky piece of work who called it as he saw it no matter how awkward it rendered the situation. In fact, he seemed to get some kind of pleasure out of making her uncomfortable.

She'd do her best to steer clear of him for the duration of the wedding.

She hated the disappointment that swirled inside her. Because she wanted another taste of Alejandro's lips—she wanted more than just another taste of his lips, if she was honest. But she also knew that the only thing she should be focusing on this week was making sure she got Sophie to the wedding and down the aisle. The conflict tugged at the outer reaches of her subconscious, and she shoved it out of her mind.

She stared up at the gorgeous stained-glass ceiling, taking a deep breath and trying to ground herself. She took her cell phone out of her pocket and checked the time. It was almost eight thirty. There were no calls from her sisters. Dana and Monica were supposed to join them for brunch at eleven, which gave Olivia two and a half hours to find Sophie and make amends.

She called Sophie's cell again. After one ring, the call went directly to voice mail.

She did not leave a message. Instead, she texted her.

Where are you, Sophie? We're worried about you. I understand why you're upset and I'm sorry. I really am, but please let us know where you are...that you're safe.

Fully expecting the message to sit unanswered, Olivia shoved her phone into the back pocket of her jeans and made her way toward the elevators. As she waited for the doors to open in the lobby, her cell phone dinged.

Olivia's heart leaped when she saw that Sophie had replied.

I'm safe.

With shaking hands, Olivia typed:

Where are you?

She stared at her phone as if she could will her sister to answer. But by the time the elevator arrived, Sophie still hadn't replied.

Olivia tried to pacify herself with the thought that maybe there was no cell service in the elevator hallway. She walked back into the lobby and typed another message.

Thank you for letting us know you're okay. Will you please meet me for a cup of coffee before the brunch so we can talk about this?

There's no need. I'm going to pass on brunch. Please give my regrets to Dana.

She was going to pass on brunch?

What am I supposed to say to Dana?

Tell the truth. Tell her I'm not getting married.

I'm going to call you. Please pick up.

There's nothing to talk about.

Are you kidding me? I worked my butt off to give you and Dana a nice weekend. You can't just opt out without so much as a phone conversation. I don't care if you thought I was a little harsh last night. Sophie, you need to grow up. Your deciding not to get married affects others besides yourself.

Seconds after she sent the message her phone rang. It was Sophie.

"Hi," Olivia said. "Thank you for calling me."

"Say what you need to say." Sophie sounded like she was crying and Olivia's heart broke a little more.

"Sophie, please, you can't take to heart what I said last night." She moved out of the lobby and into the bar area where they were last night, looking for a quiet corner where she could talk to her sister privately. "Please don't let my cynical drunken words cause you to make the worst mistake of your life."

"Those weren't just liquor-inspired words, Liv. It's the truth. Every single word of what you said is true. Are you trying to tell me it's not?"

It was true. Her parents had a terrible marriage. If you could even call it a marriage. They led separate lives because they couldn't stand each other.

"I thought so," Sophie said on a sob when Olivia didn't reply. "Look, I need some time to figure out what I'm going to do. I appreciate all the time and hard work you put into the bachelorette party, but I need some space right now. I hope you understand."

"What do you want me to tell Dana?"

Sophie was inconsolable. It killed Olivia to hear her sister in so much pain. Especially since she was the one who'd caused it.

"Tell her whatever you want, Liv. I have to go."

"No, Sophie. Please tell me where you are—"

But it was too late. Her sister had already disconnected the call.

Olivia stood there trying to get her bearings, trying to figure out how to fix this mess—and quickly. It was best not to push Sophie about the brunch. Olivia kicked herself for scheduling the bachelorette party the weekend before the wedding. She should've done this last month. Sophie wasn't a partier and she was probably exhausted and overwhelmed by all the hoopla leading up to her wedding day. The best thing Olivia could do right now was to show her sister some compassion, give her the space she so clearly needed.

They'd simply tell Dana and Monica that Sophie was under the weather. Given the Fuzzy Handcuffs, that wouldn't be such a stretch.

As Olivia made her way upstairs to tell Zoe and Rachel that she'd talked to Sophie, she saw Mason at the front desk.

She called out to him and steeled herself for a frantic response from the bridegroom, but Mason smiled at her, appearing remarkably calm.

"Hey, Liv. What's the latest?"

Good old Mason, the calm to Sophie's occasional dramatic storm. She said a silent prayer that they would be able to weather this Category Five. How, exactly, did one explain that his fiancée was possibly backing out of the wedding? Then, in a moment of clarity, Olivia realized that even if her careless words had set off Sophie, it was Sophie's responsibility to tell Mason she wanted to call things off, not hers.

Olivia put on her bravest face. "I just got off the phone with Sophie. Have you spoken to her?"

"Not yet." Mason pulled out his cell phone. "I'll text her and tell her I'm talking to you."

Olivia waited and watched as Mason sent a message. Sophie responded immediately but it was a good two minutes before Mason finally looked up and said,

"What we have here is a good old-fashioned case of cold feet. She'll be fine. Just give her a little bit of time."

Mason's calm was rubbing off on Olivia. Still, she made sure she had her filter firmly in place before she spoke. She had learned her lesson after last night. The less said the better.

"I figure until she feels better, we can simply tell people she's got a bug," Mason said, looking so confident. "That's all they need to know."

"Sure," Olivia echoed. "That's all they need to know."

In the meantime, Olivia silently vowed, she would fix this mess.

She uttered a silent prayer that she could pull it off.

Chapter Three

On Monday evening, Alejandro handed the rental car keys to the valet parking attendant outside the Robinson estate and accepted his claim check. He'd been to functions at the sprawling estate when his brothers, Matteo and Joaquin, had married Rachel and Zoe, but the magnitude of its grandeur still rendered him awestruck.

The place made a statement about who Gerald Robinson was and what he stood for: a man who had started with nothing and built himself an empire with his brainchild, Robinson Computers. The man was brilliant. Alejandro might have found him intimidating if he hadn't been so intriguing. As an entrepreneur himself, Alejandro devoured biographies of successful businesspeople. Seeing how someone else created an empire was better than any business course he could take.

He would've been lying if he'd denied wanting all of this for himself. He wanted it so badly he could taste it.

Someday, he thought, as his shoes hit the pavers of the cobblestone path that was lined with tiki torches and directed people to the back of this castle of a house.

"Aloha. Good evening." Two attractive women dressed in loose-fitting Hawaiian-print dresses greeted Alejandro with warm smiles. Both had tucked a white flower into their long, dark hair. The print of their matching dresses reminded him of a shirt he used to wear back in his college days—only it looked much classier on them.

"Welcome to the wedding luau," the one holding a lei said.

She stepped forward and placed it around his neck and her dark hair glistened in the golden tiki-torch light, reminding him of Olivia and the unfortunate way they'd parted. He regretted grilling her the way he had yesterday morning. As soon as she'd walked away, he'd been planning his apology. He'd been out of line debating her sister's obviously fragile state. He knew it, he owned it and he would apologize for it. He didn't want anything to detract from the wedding festivities—certainly not bad blood or resentment stemming from yesterday's disagreement. Or Saturday night's kiss, either.

All day, the two events had played tug-of-war in

his mind. He'd had to hyperfocus during his business meeting at Hummingbird Ridge. It was a rare occasion when he allowed anything to distract him from business. But he hadn't exactly invited Olivia into his brain. She'd barged in unbidden, as strong a presence when she wasn't in the room as when they were standing face-to-face.

As soon as the woman who had presented him with the lei stepped away, her cohort stepped forward and offered him a drink served in a hollowed-out pineapple. The beverage was adorned with exotic flowers, a blue plastic straw and a tiny umbrella.

He took a sip. The rum and tropical fruit juices combined for a delicious drink. The Fortune Robinsons seemed to have cornered the market on signature cocktails. He certainly wasn't complaining since he was on the receiving end of all this libation creativity.

But since signature cocktails and Olivia Fortune Robinson had proven to be a rather explosive combination, he decided he needed to exercise the utmost caution tonight. Then again, given Olivia's demeanor the last time he saw her, he probably didn't have to worry.

The woman who had handed him the drink gestured to her right. "Please follow the torch-lined path around to the tent on the rear lawn and enjoy the festivities."

"Thank you," he said, raising his pineapple in an appreciative toast.

He followed the path and the sound of music. As he rounded the corner and the tent came into view, he took a deep breath and inhaled the sweet scent of gardenias mingling with delicious, smoky BBQ and firewood burning in outdoor fireplaces. A crowd of people mingled on the manicured lawn as a country band played on a stage in front of a parquet dance floor that had been laid out on the grounds.

Alejandro's gaze scanned the crowd for familiar faces. His stomach growled and he realized he hadn't eaten since breakfast. The meeting with the fine folks of Hummingbird Ridge had lasted through the lunch hour. He'd taken some time to drive around the area to get a feel for the town, which was located about a half hour west of Austin. Once he'd returned to the hotel, he'd been tied up on calls with investors, bankers and his partners—his cousins Stefan and Rodrigo Mendoza. Before he knew it, he'd had just enough time to shower, shave and get dressed for tonight.

Skipping lunch was a small price to pay because today he had taken another step toward creating his own empire. The trip out to Hummingbird Ridge had proven that the winery and its acres of thriving vineyards were, indeed, a good investment. The Texas Hill Country was one of the country's upcoming wine destinations.

Alejandro's interest in the wine business had started as a fluke. When he was in college at the University of Florida, he used to come home for the summer. Between his freshman and sophomore years, he'd taken a summer job at a South Beach wine bar to save money for tuition. What he'd thought would be a fleeting means to an end had sparked a passion in him, triggering him to change his major to agricultural operations and eventually get a master's degree in viticulture and enology. Not only had he learned the complexities and distinctions the different grape varietals lent to the bottled end product, he'd become educated on theories such as *terroir*—how the climate and land of an area worked together to make wines unique. He had spent a summer in France interning at a vineyard and another summer at a winery in the Napa Valley. Winemaking fascinated him, but he'd known if he wanted to make enough money to one day buy his own vineyard, he needed to be in sales. After scrimping and saving and working his ass off for a decade, his dream was close to becoming a reality. In fact, it was so close he could almost taste the wine.

Alejandro accepted a bacon-wrapped scallop off an hors d'oeuvre platter passed by a server dressed in Polynesian garb. As he bit into it, he continued to scan the crowd for familiar faces. Hundreds of friends and relatives had started to trickle in for the week of prewedding festivities outlined in the itinerary he'd received when he'd checked in at the Driskill. The information packet had included a schedule of events with dates and times for romantic couples' massages, rounds of golf and dinners. If nothing else, they would be entertained and well fed while they were here.

He hadn't forgotten his promise to check into the logistics of an informal wine tasting at Hummingbird Ridge. Even if the wedding party couldn't fit it into their schedule, which was pretty packed, it would be a great opportunity to spend some time with his father, his brothers and their wives. The Mendozas were a close-knit bunch and he didn't get a chance to see his siblings much now that they were married. His three brothers, Cisco, Matteo, Joaquin, their sister, Gabriella, and their dad, Orlando, had traded in Miami and moved to Texas. If everything panned out with the winery, Alejandro might be following suit, or at the very least visiting more often.

Before Alejandro could locate his family—his brothers and father were there, but his sister, Gabi, and her husband, Jude Fortune Jones, would arrive Saturday morning for the wedding—Kieran Fortune Robinson and Dana joined the band onstage. Kieran accepted the microphone from the guitar player.

"Good evening, everyone," Kieran said. "On behalf of my beautiful fiancée, Dana, my little sister Sophie and her fiancé, Mason, I'd like to welcome you to the start of our wedding week celebration. We are so glad you could join us as we count down the days leading up to the big event. Unfortunately, Sophie is a little under the weather tonight. She stayed home to rest up so that she'll be back to one hundred percent for Saturday."

Alejandro flinched as he recalled Olivia's frantic search for Sophie yesterday morning. Olivia had been so certain that her sister would be fine that Alejandro hadn't even considered the possibility that Sophie might not be here this evening. Was she still having second thoughts about the wedding?

Obviously Kieran and Dana's nuptials were still on. Alejandro watched the couple kiss when the crowd interrupted Kieran's welcoming remarks with chants of "Kiss her! Kiss her! Kiss her!" Kieran grabbed Dana and rocked her back as he planted a smooch on her lips.

The spectacle reminded him of kissing Olivia Saturday night at the Driskill Hotel. He immediately shook away the image, because thoughts like that could only lead to trouble.

Instead, he trained his focus on Kieran and Dana, who looked so happy together. Alejandro understood how they felt; he'd been there before, a long time ago. Were they so caught up in their own happiness they didn't know that Sophie was having second thoughts? Then again, for all he knew, maybe Olivia had found her sister and everything was just fine. Maybe she really was under the weather and the illness was what had driven her away from the Driskill Sunday morning.

Obviously he needed to find a friend here at the party if he'd been reduced to standing here alone pondering situations that had nothing to do with him.

"Please, help yourself to some barbecue and the open bar," Kieran said once he and Dana had come up for air. "In fact, if everyone could grab a drink, I would like to make a toast."

Olivia had groaned when Kieran had dipped Dana back in that shameless public display of affection. She'd groaned and then she'd been ashamed of herself. She'd wished she could take back the ugly sound as she'd glanced around to see if anyone had heard her.

They hadn't.

Of course not. Everyone was too busy *oohing* and *ahhing* over the blithe display of love. Good grief. Her brother had no shame.

As inappropriate as the groan had been, what she'd really wanted to do was shout *Get a room!* She'd been tempted, but she'd never actually do it. The groan had been the slightly less inappropriate compromise. Her attempt at good party manners.

Right.

She wanted to be happy for Kieran and Dana—and she was. Really, she was. But she was so wrecked over Sophie not being here tonight that her guilt was pretty much all-consuming.

She wished she could borrow some confidence from Mason. He loved Sophie so much and he was determined to stand by her while she figured out her heart.

Mason was willing to fight for Sophie's love—even if that fight entailed him attending the barbe-cue solo and keeping up the cover that Sophie was home sick with the flu and would be good as new by Saturday. His resolute love made Olivia do a mental double take. No one had ever been willing to fight for her like that. Every person she'd ever allowed her-self to feel anything substantial for had walked away when the going had gotten tough. Most of the men who had hurt her—two of them in particular—had been more interested in cozying up to her father, who they'd believed could help them get ahead. When that didn't pan out, they'd left. No one had ever fought for her or believed in her the way Mason believed in Sophie. Sophie and Mason had something special and while it didn't alter Olivia's own thoughts on love, she was willing to concede that her little sister might have actually lassoed the unicorn.

Men like Mason were rare, almost mythical, and Olivia wasn't about to let Sophie make the biggest mistake of her life by letting Mason get away.

Even so, with Sophie refusing to attend the party tonight, Olivia was enough of a realist to know that nothing short of a miracle was going to change her sister's mind. Nothing less than Olivia being struck by lightning…or cupid's arrow. But that wasn't going to happen. She needed to come up with another plan.

Olivia racked her brain, but she kept coming back to one thing. Cupid's arrow. She had a feeling that the only way she was going to make amends with Sophie was by convincing her that she believed in love, that somehow, overnight, she'd had a total change of heart. It was crazy, but it might work. What did she have to lose? Olivia had to take action or otherwise risk earning the title of Prewedding Homewrecker— and carrying around the guilt from being responsible for ruining Sophie's life.

But how in the world could she pull it off? How could she make her sister believe she thought true love was possible?

Olivia was in full panic mode as she scanned the

crowd of guests who had gathered for the barbecue, as if the answer lay in the midst of people—both familiar and those she'd never met—who were enjoying the hors d'oeuvres and raising glasses in anticipation of Kieran's toast and in honor of the soon-to-be newlyweds.

Her gaze lit on her sister Rachel, who was talking to her husband, Matteo. Next to them, Zoe was flirting with her husband, Joaquin. There, like a very handsome third wheel, stood Alejandro, bedecked in an orchid lei and holding his pineapple cup.

The last single Mendoza.

Olivia's mind replayed the kiss they'd shared on Saturday night. In an instant her lips tingled as the feel and taste of him came flooding back, as if he'd kissed her only a moment ago.

That kiss... That. Kiss.

Suddenly, she was struck by a bolt of sexy inspiration. The idea was crazy—and a little bit naughty— but it just might work. As long as Alejandro went along with her plan.

Servers appeared with trays of champagne flutes. As Kieran gave the guests a moment to arm themselves with libations, Alejandro sensed someone standing too close behind him, invading his personal space. Before he could turn around a pair of feminine arms encircled his waist and a sultry voice that sounded a lot like Olivia's whispered in his ear.

"I know this sounds crazy, but I need you to kiss

me right here, right now, and make it look real. Please just go along with it and don't ask questions."

Was this some kind of a joke?

"What?"

She didn't answer him. She simply moved around so that she was standing directly in front of him. She took the pineapple drink from his hand and set it on the tray of a passing server then she cupped his face in her hands and laid one on him with the same ferocity she'd shown Saturday night.

As she opened her mouth, inviting him deep inside, he obliged. And the rest of the world—and all the questions that had popped into his head as Olivia had whispered her request—faded away. Alejandro pulled her in flush with his body and did exactly as she had asked. There would be plenty of time for questions later. Right now her wish was his command.

The kiss was a lightning bolt that seared Alejandro to his core. He wasn't sure how long they'd stood there, lip to lip, locked in each other's arms, breathing each other's air, but he was vaguely aware of distant cheering as he and Olivia slowly broke the kiss and separated. People were, in fact, cheering, and it wasn't for Kieran and Dana. Everyone who was standing near them was looking at them.

Everyone except for his brothers. Cisco, Matteo and Joaquin weren't cheering; they were piercing him with looks that screamed *What the hell are you doing?*

What the hell *was* he doing?

That was all it took to sober him up. But then Olivia, who still had her arms draped around his neck, leaned in and whispered, "Thank you. Please just keep up the act. I'll explain as soon as we're alone."

Alejandro understood that her version of being alone probably wouldn't include more kissing. But that wasn't the most pressing problem at the moment.

"Quiet down, everyone," Kieran instructed the buzzing crowd. "Olivia, is there anything you'd like to tell us?"

All eyes turned to Olivia, who still had her arms draped over his shoulders. She just smiled sweetly and made a show of shrugging in a noncommittal way that only fed the fire of speculation.

What *was* she doing? She seemed too smart and sure of herself to be unstable. Olivia clearly knew what she was doing. She was up to something and she was pulling him into it. Yesterday, she was arguing with him and asserting that they needed to act like the kiss had never happened, that everyone would be better off if they kept their distance from each other. Then today she was stealing her brother's thunder and making a spectacle of kissing him senseless.

"Should we start making plans to accommodate a third bride and groom?" Kieran said into the microphone.

As Olivia turned toward her brother, her arm dropped to Alejandro's waist and she held on. He followed suit, putting his arm around her.

One of the servers appeared in front of them with a tray of champagne flutes. They both took one.

"This is your night, my dear brother. Yours, Dana's, Sophie's and Mason's," she said. "To you and to your love and happiness."

The crowd cheered again and raised pineapple drinks and champagne flutes in tribute. The collective attention shifted back to Kieran and Dana.

"Thanks, sis," Kieran said. "That was a perfect toast. I couldn't have said it better." He sipped his champagne. "We hope everyone enjoys this magical week with us. Obviously we're off to a great start." He gestured with his head toward Olivia.

Alejandro felt a little uneasy being dragged into the spotlight. He was happy helping Olivia with whatever she was trying to accomplish—especially if it involved kissing her—but he'd prefer to know what he was working toward.

As everyone settled back into their groups and others made their way toward the food, Rachel, Matteo, Joaquin and Zoe cornered them.

"Hello?" Zoe said. "I think the two of you have some explaining to do."

"What do you mean?" Olivia asked. Alejandro both admired and resented her poker face. He wanted an explanation, too.

"Um, this?" Zoe gestured back and forth between Olivia and Alejandro with her manicured fingers. "When did this happen? What exactly is happening? And when were you going to tell us?"

Alejandro gazed down at Olivia. This was all her

show. He smiled the message to her when she glanced up at him, looking every bit like the smitten lover.

Without missing a beat, Olivia said, "Surprise! We just sort of fell into this. Isn't it great?"

As the quartet uttered sounds of confused surprise, Alejandro said, "Yes, we just couldn't resist each other."

Spoken aloud, the sentiment didn't quite sound as convincing as it had in his head.

"Will you excuse us for a minute?" he said before he could say anything else inane. "Olivia and I were getting ready to—"

Getting ready to what?

"We were getting ready to take a tour of the house," Olivia said. "Come on, sweetheart. Let's do that now so we can get back and have dinner."

As Olivia slid her hand into his, Alejandro said, "Excuse us. We'll be right back."

They walked hand in hand in silence, across the lush green lawn to stone steps that led past the pool to a travertine porch. Alejandro looked back at the grounds and the lake that bordered the massive property.

"Is that Lake Austin?" he asked.

"It is," she said as she opened the back door and they stepped inside the house. Alejandro thought they'd be alone once they were inside, but staff milled about everywhere, carrying platters of food and drink and working purposefully. The buzz inside the house, coupled with the sheer grandeur of the place, stunned him into silence.

Alejandro did not speak another word until Olivia had shut them inside a room on the second floor. It was larger than his first apartment.

He blinked as Olivia flicked on a light. The expensive-looking feminine decor registered on him. "Is this your bedroom?"

"It is," she said. "Or it used to be. I have my own place now."

"It's nice that your folks kept it the way you left it. You know, that they didn't turn it into an exercise room or a man cave."

Olivia shrugged. "The house has always had a gym and my father has three man caves. My parents aren't sacrificing anything by keeping my space intact. It's not as if they kept it like this as a shrine to me. It's just not beneficial for them to change it. You know, it was easier to just shut the door. But that's not why I dragged you up here."

She bit her bottom lip again, pulling it into her mouth, a gesture he was beginning to associate with her pensive side.

"Did you bring me in here to make out?" he joked.

"No, I didn't." The sharpness of her tone shouldn't have surprised him, but it did.

He crossed his arms. "Would you care to share why you felt compelled to put on that display out there? You made it look like you couldn't wait to jump my bones."

She looked visibly deflated, but she nodded toward a black chair situated across from a plush sofa and a glass coffee table. The decor looked like it could've been featured in one of those designer house magazines. The sleek, sophisticated, expensive look of it perfectly reflected Olivia's own style.

After they'd seated themselves, she confessed, "I do owe you an explanation and a debt of gratitude. I just don't quite know how to say this. And before I say anything, I need you to swear on your family's life that you can keep a secret. Because if one word of this gets out, it would be very hurtful to certain members of my family."

He made a cross over his heart with his right hand. "I would offer to stick a needle in my eye, but I don't like needles."

She cocked a dark brow. "What? A big, strong, tough guy like you is afraid of needles? I don't believe it."

He wanted to say that needles didn't scare him nearly as much as she did. It was becoming clear that she addled his brain so much that she was able to lord some kind of power over him.

"Look, this has nothing to do with needles," he said. "Why don't you just tell me what's going on? Why did you kiss me like that out there?"

"I did it because I need everyone to believe we're in love—or that I'm in love with you. No, it would be better if they believed that we love each other, you know, mutually."

"But, Olivia, you don't love me. Why do you want everyone to think you do tonight, when yesterday you made it clear that me kissing you again was strictly forbidden? Because it would detract from the wedding, take the focus off the brides and grooms?"

When she didn't answer him, he said, "You're a beautiful woman. You're smart and funny and you're a hell of a good kisser, but I'm starting to think you're off your rocker."

"Oh, well, there you go," Olivia said. "For a second there I was tempted to think you were paying me a compliment. You know, calling me a beautiful woman."

"I was. You are. But I'm a little confused here. I was prepared to make the sacrifice of never kissing you again—for the greater good, for your sister's happiness, but—"

"You wanted to kiss me again, Alejandro?"

"Of course I did."

"Oh. That's good. Then how do you feel about being my pretend lover for the duration of the wedding? You know, my boyfriend—or my intensely romantic date. No, it needs to be more than just a date. I need for Sophie to believe that I've fallen in love with you. I messed up big-time Saturday night. Because of my big mouth, my sister has lost all faith in love. I figure the only way to undo the damage I've caused is by making her believe that I've had a change of heart about love. It's the only way to renew her faith. Would you be willing to do that for me... for my sister?" She suddenly looked very small and fragile, but she looked at him intently. "I promise I will make it worth your while."

Now it was his turn to cock a brow and mess

with her. "And just how would you make it worth
my while? Can you please be more specific? I'm talking details. The more vivid the better."

His mouth crooked up on one side and she obviously caught his drift because her cheeks flushed the
same color as the hot-pink area rug under their feet.

"Certainly not in the way I think you're implying.
You have a dirty mind, Alejandro."

"Hey, I didn't say a word. I was thinking along the
lines of dancing and being dinner partners. So the
hordes of adoring women will think I'm taken and
leave me alone." He was smiling so that she would
know he was joking. "That's what I was thinking.
However, I am not responsible for whatever that mind
of yours conjures up. If you'd like to try out your
thoughts and see if it works for you, I'm happy to be
at your service."

Her mouth fell open and he could tell she was trying to feign disgust, but the pretense hadn't reached
her eyes. "Why are you making this so difficult?"

"Because watching you squirm is so much fun."
He held her gaze as he grappled with a peculiar feeling in the pit of his stomach. Something he hadn't felt
in ages. Interest and attraction. Maybe this wedding
was going to be more interesting than he'd thought.
At the very least, it would be fun.

He'd go along as her pretend boyfriend. It wasn't
as if he was agreeing to marry her.

He shrugged, to appear not too eager. "I guess I've
had worse offers," he said. "I'd be happy to play the

role of your lover for the duration of the wedding."
But he couldn't resist needling her a bit. "Just how
deeply into character would you like to go?"

Chapter Four

"You pride yourself on being the king of the innuendo, don't you?" Olivia said, exercising great restraint to resist adding another layer to his insinuation. The chemistry between them begged her to keep the banter going, to tell him she was all about method acting and she was at his service for any research he needed in order to deliver a convincing performance.

Actually, her body was all in for the research, but her brain knew better. They needed to keep this strictly aboveboard.

"That's the thing about innuendo," he said. "You can interpret it however you choose."

"Okay, since you put it that way, I'd love an Oscar-winning performance, but we need to keep this act strictly PG."

He frowned. "That's disappointing. I was thinking an R-rated production would be so much more convincing."

"Sorry to disappoint you, Romeo, but let's not get carried away. Need I remind you that while this show we're about to put on is a limited engagement, we'll still have to stage a breakup and coexist at future family functions."

He frowned.

"It's not like we'll have to sit across the dinner table from each other every Sunday," he said.

"True."

Maybe this wasn't a good idea. Was it fair to ask a guy she barely knew to pretend to be her lover? To play the part convincingly without giving him all access? For a fleeting moment, she let herself go there. What if for one careless week she allowed herself to go off the rails and immerse herself in the part—onstage and off?

"What are you getting at, Alejandro? Do you expect me to sleep with you?"

After she set the words free, released them from the cage in her mind, the prospect of letting go like that was petrifying. She might not believe in love, but she did believe in feelings. And feelings, when you allowed them to meander unchecked, made you susceptible to hurt.

No. If there was ever a time that she needed to stay completely in control it was now. This was about Sophie. It wasn't about her. It was a means to an end to fix what she had nearly broken.

"You make it sound so romantic," Alejandro said.

When she didn't jab back, he seemed to ease up. "It's clear that's not what you want. So, no, I don't expect you to sleep with me. I would never use sex as a bartering chip. Don't worry, Olivia. You're safe with me."

She should've been relieved, but the most primitive part of her was disappointed that sex was off the table. But she reminded herself that she needed to set the ground rules up front and they needed to stick to them. For their own good. Hadn't the Sophie disaster been enough of a cautionary tale of what happened when she got careless?

"That's good to know," she said. "I'm glad we're on the same page."

He nodded, but things still felt off-kilter. Before they left this room, she needed to make sure everything was as right as it could be.

"Please know that I do appreciate you helping me," she said. "It's good of you, Alejandro. I realize you don't have to do this. I mean, Sophie is my sister. I'm the one who opened my big mouth and set everything spinning out of control."

Olivia clamped her mouth shut. She was talking too much. She always did when she felt out of control. Obviously she needed to admit to herself that Alejandro Mendoza made her feel that way. *Yes, just acknowledge it—look the problem in the eye, stare it down—and move on.*

She locked gazes with him. Looked deep into those brown eyes, straight into the lighter brown and golden flecks that she hadn't noticed before. He was the first one to blink, breaking the trance, but she still didn't feel any more in control than before she'd tried to stare down the dragon. She needed to try another tactic.

"Even though I'm appreciative and I shouldn't question your motives, I'm wondering why you would do this for me."

There. She'd said it. And it needed to be said.

He was frowning at her again. Not an affected frown this time, but a genuine look of consternation. Still, she was glad she'd said it. Knowing what he was expecting in return for helping her might put things on a bit more of a level playing field.

"What's in this for me." It wasn't a question. The way he repeated her words was more like he was turning them around, looking at them from all angles. "What's in this for me. I don't know, Olivia. Should I expect personal gain? Because I wasn't, other than maybe the satisfaction of helping you out."

"Look, Alejandro, I didn't mean that in the way you seem to be taking it. I just wanted to make sure we're both laying all our cards on the table before we go any further."

"Is everything a business venture to you? I get the feeling you're about to whip out a contract for me to sign."

She wished it was that easy. For a terrifying moment, she feared that her plan was a mistake.

She stood. "I'm sorry. Let's just forget about this whole thing and proceed with business as usual between us. It's not you…it was a bad idea."

He reached out and took her hand, tugging her gently to get her to sit back down. And, of course, she did. Because it was clear that her better judgment, which was telling her to run away and save herself, went belly up when Alejandro did so much as breathe near her. With this man she felt totally out of control. And it was petrifying.

"I hate to be the voice of reality, but after that show we put on before the toast, people are going to have questions. And even though I don't know your sister very well, if everything you said is true—and I have no reason to believe it's not—do you think it will restore Sophie's faith if word gets back to her that it's 'business as usual' between us again?"

The guy was more insightful than she'd given him credit for. And he was absolutely right. Sophie would be completely disheartened, and with good reason. There was no backing out now unless she wanted to put the final nail in the coffin on Sophie's desire to marry.

"You're right," she told him. "You're a good man to allow me to drag you into this, Alejandro. I promise I'll make it up to you somehow."

"I'll hold you to that." He reached out and took her hand. Only this time it felt different. Not as dangerous, even though the butterflies in her stomach still flew in formation.

"Shall we go back to the party? I think we have some explaining to do."

He smiled. "Let the show begin."

Olivia should've known she wouldn't be able to fool her sisters. She shouldn't have even tried. But even though they'd gone along with the charade at the party, pretending to be just as surprised and convinced as everyone else by her love affair with Alejandro, Zoe and Rachel had shown up at her condo early the next morning with a box of doughnuts and plenty of questions.

She'd spilled the beans within the first five minutes.

"So we weren't convincing?" Olivia asked as she put the kettle on to boil water for coffee in the French press. "Please, at least tell me we weren't painfully obvious."

"You were absolutely convincing to the untrained eye," Rachel said as she took down coffee mugs from the cabinet above the stove. "You should know better than to try to pull one over on Zoe and me. Why didn't you tell us about the plan from the start?"

Olivia turned toward her sisters and braced the small of her back against the edge of the counter.

"I didn't have a plan per se. In fact, when I saw that Sophie hadn't snapped out of her funk by last night, I was in full panic mode. She missed the brunch and then the dinner where she was supposed to welcome her guests. It was starting to feel like something more than cold feet. I'm afraid if it goes on much longer,

Mason won't be able to keep up her flu cover-up. Either that, or he's going to lose his patience. I mean, how would you all feel if your husbands had ditched the wedding events and told you they weren't sure they wanted to marry you less than a week before the wedding?"

Her sisters nodded in agreement.

"Thank goodness Mason is a very patient man," said Rachel. "So what are you planning to do? Are you counting on word of your affair with Alejandro magically getting back to Sophie? Or do you have a plan?"

Olivia bought herself some time by grinding the coffee beans she had measured out. It only took a few seconds, but by the time she'd finished, both of her sisters were staring at her expectantly, waiting for an answer.

"I definitely want to be proactive," Olivia said. "There's not enough time to leave matters up to chance. However, before I can do anything I need to figure out where she is. I haven't talked to her since Sunday. Have either of you heard from her?"

Olivia already knew the answer to that question. Because of course her sisters would've rushed to her the minute they had learned Sophie's whereabouts. No, this was a code red situation. And they needed to do something to avert a major catastrophe. Since the three of them were together and would soon be fortified by doughnuts, she was confident they'd come up with something.

Zoe cleared her throat as if she had something to

say. That's when it dawned on Olivia that her sister had been uncharacteristically quiet as she and Rachel had been mulling over the situation.

"I know where Sophie is," Zoe said.

The tea kettle whistled as if punctuating Olivia's agitation.

"What? Where is she?" Olivia demanded as she took the kettle off the flame.

Zoe stood there silently, looking away from her sisters.

"You've been standing here all this time harboring this information?" Rachel said. "Are you going to make us pry it out of you, or are you going to tell us?"

Zoe shot daggers at Rachel. "She asked me not to tell."

"Honey, this is not an ordinary situation," Olivia said. "You're not betraying her trust by telling us. In fact, you just might be saving her marriage. Where is she?"

"I still can't believe she's been right here the whole time," Olivia said as she and her sisters climbed the stairs of their childhood home. "She was probably watching the party last night from her window. Alejandro and I were right down the hall from her."

Olivia stopped in her tracks causing Rachel to nearly bump into her. "Oh my gosh. I hope she didn't overhear Alejandro and me talking."

"I don't think so," Zoe whispered. "I spoke to her last night and she didn't say anything. And you know she would've had plenty to say if she'd heard you."

"Good point," Olivia whispered back. "Let's—" She drew a finger over her throat in a gesture that meant *silence* and motioned for them to continue on to Sophie's room.

The three sisters traveled quietly down the long hall. Sophie's room was at the opposite end of the hall from Olivia's. She was grateful because if her sister had overheard the conversation it would have made matters even worse. Now, regardless of how dangerous the Alejandro plan felt, it was her last recourse. It had to work, because she certainly didn't have a plan B.

Nor did she have a plan for approaching her sister, she realized when they finally stood in front of Sophie's bedroom door. Zoe and Rachel looked at Olivia, as if they were waiting for her to do something. So she did what she did best and took charge. She gestured to Zoe, indicating that she should knock on the door and be the one to speak to Sophie first.

At first, Zoe shook her head, but through a series of pantomimes Olivia was able to impart that it was only logical for Zoe to be the one to knock because she was the only one who knew Sophie was here. With a resigned shrug Zoe acquiesced and gave the door a tentative rap.

"Sophie?" she said. "Are you in there? It's me, Zoe. I just wanted to check on you. See how you are."

When she didn't answer, Olivia tried the door. It was locked. Olivia motioned for Zoe to knock again. This time Zoe didn't argue.

"Come on, Soph. Open up. Please? You can't hide

in here forever. Besides, it's getting kind of difficult to explain your absence to the guests. You're gonna have to make up your mind about what you want to do. You owe Mason that much."

Olivia gave Zoe the signal to tone it down a little bit. She appreciated what her sister was trying to do, but she was still holding out hope that the soft touch might work.

As if reading Olivia's mind, Zoe changed her tactic. "Besides, if you don't open the door I'm not going to tell you the gossip. And it's juicy. It involves Alejandro Mendoza. You're definitely going to want to hear this."

Sophie almost caught Olivia giving Zoe the thumbs-up. Because the tidbit about Alejandro seemed to be the magic words that made Sophie open the door for Zoe.

Of course, when she saw Rachel and Olivia standing there too, she tried to shut the door again, but the three of them were quicker than Sophie and managed to muscle their way in before she could lock them out.

Before Sophie could say anything, her sisters grabbed her in a four-way group hug as they cooed their concern and happiness about finally seeing her again.

"We were so worried about you," Rachel said.

"How are you doing?" Olivia asked.

"Have you changed your mind about the wedding?" Zoe asked. "Are you getting married?"

All Sophie could say was "I don't know. I don't know what I believe anymore."

Olivia noticed that Sophie didn't utter one word of protest about Zoe's sharing the secret of her whereabouts. That confirmed what Olivia had suspected—that Sophie had told Zoe because she knew Zoe wouldn't be able to keep the secret.

Zoe was the loose lips, Rachel was the vault and Olivia was the problem solver.

"You said there was gossip?" Sophie asked. "About Alejandro Mendoza?"

Olivia felt relief—her sister seemed to be playing right into their hands. Good thing, too, because Olivia didn't know how they would have steered her in that direction if she hadn't brought it up herself.

Olivia said a silent prayer that Zoe would pick up on her cue and proceed in a way that didn't look staged.

"Oh, that's not important," Olivia feigned. "We are here to talk to you, to see what we can do to make you feel better about everything."

Olivia held her breath.

"The best thing you could do for me right now is to talk about something other than the wedding. Because if you keep badgering me about it, you can't stay." Sophie walked over to the door and put her hand on the knob as if she were demonstrating how she would show them out.

"Then you're saying we can stay if we don't talk about the wedding?" Rachel asked.

Sophie eyed her sisters as if she were weighing the pros and cons.

"Olivia and Alejandro hooked up last night." Zoe

spat the words so perfectly Olivia had to remind herself to look suitably offended. After all, if this had been a true hookup, she wouldn't have wanted anyone—even her sisters—gossiping about it.

The ploy seemed to be working, because Sophie's jaw dropped and her eyes were huge.

"Zoe," Olivia admonished, "you promised you wouldn't say anything."

Rachel rolled her eyes. "Well, you two made such a spectacle of yourselves last night that if Sophie didn't hear it from Zoe she would certainly hear about it from someone else."

Olivia stood there silently, channeling her best humiliated/indignant expression.

"This is nobody's business but mine and Alejandro's," Olivia said. "So just stop, okay?"

"Oh, I don't think so," said Sophie. Her eyes sparkled as she took the bait—hook, line and sinker. She grabbed Olivia's arm and tugged her toward the couch by the window. "You are not leaving until you tell me everything."

She looked at Zoe and Rachel. "This happened last night? At the welcome barbecue? And I missed it?"

Zoe and Rachel nodded, a little too enthusiastically.

"Yep. You missed it," Zoe said. "If you would've been there last night you would've had a front-row seat."

No. If she'd been there last night nothing would've happened. There would've been no need.

Olivia's mind replayed last night's kiss. The details

were so vivid she could virtually feel Alejandro's lips on hers. Never in her life had she been at odds with herself like she was over this. Every womanly cell in her body couldn't wait for her to kiss him again, but every ounce of common sense in her brain reminded her to rein it in. Because if the plan worked like it seemed to be working, she was going to be kissing Alejandro a lot more. It was fine if she enjoyed it. In fact, it was probably for the best if she did since they'd be spending so much time together. However, it was in her own best interest to not get carried away.

"Olivia! Oh, my gosh," Sophie squealed. "He's gorgeous, and I knew he was interested in you because of the way he was looking at you Saturday night. Did I call it or what?" She looked at Zoe and Rachel. "I called it. Didn't I call it?"

Sophie clapped her hands gleefully, looking like she'd just opened the front door and found the prize patrol of a sweepstakes holding a big check made out to her.

"You called it, Soph," Rachel conceded.

Olivia crossed her arms and let her body fall back against the couch with a petulant *harrumph*.

Sophie angled herself toward Olivia. "Tell me everything. Start from the beginning and tell me every juicy detail. Come on, Liv. Spill it."

Olivia looked down and shook her head. "I'm glad you all think this is entertaining, but I don't want to talk about it."

"Wait, what?" Rachel asked. "Alejandro is gorgeous and we would all like to live vicariously through you for just a few minutes. I mean, it was just a hookup. What's the harm in sharing?"

Perfect.

Olivia took a deep breath and bit her bottom lip, doing her best to look sincerely offended.

"I'm not sure it was just a hookup," she said. "So you all just hop off, okay?"

"Are you saying you care about him?" Zoe asked.

Olivia gave a one-shoulder shrug. "Yeah, I think I do."

Sophie was watching, rapt. Olivia decided she needed to kick it up a level.

"I didn't think it was possible. Really, I didn't think it would ever happen to me. I thought I was immune." She placed both of her hands over her heart. "But for the first time in my life, I think I'm in love. Truly, madly, deeply in love." One at a time, she looked each of her sisters in the eye, ending with Sophie. That's when she delivered the knockout punch. "I'm in love with Alejandro Mendoza and he feels the same way."

Sophie sat there looking stunned. When she didn't speak, Olivia feared that she'd been a little too melodramatic. Maybe the *truly, madly, deeply* bit was a little over-the-top. *Ugh,* it probably was. It was the title of her favorite Alan Rickman movie, and the name of that corny Savage Garden song, which had to be one of the sappiest love songs ever. Okay, so she'd secretly loved it ever since the time she and her sisters had gotten up and sang it at karaoke night at Señor Iguana's.

The fib had come to her in a rush, but that might

have been the reason Sophie was just sitting there staring at her. Olivia said a silent prayer hoping she hadn't blown it.

Chapter Five

Alejandro was able to arrange a wine tasting for Wednesday afternoon at Hummingbird Ridge Vineyard. It was short notice, but he was psyched when Olivia was able to herd and organize a group of fourteen who were interested in going. It was his wedding gift to the brides and grooms.

Alejandro had left the outing to the discretion of the wedding party, and the final group ended up being comprised of family—Mendozas and Fortune Robinsons. It was great, in theory. The problem was Olivia's "we're in love" plan seemed to be working, as Sophie seemed to have miraculously recovered from her "flu" and had happily agreed to join them. That meant they had to put on a convincing performance for Sophie's benefit in front of key members of the family—Mason, Dana and Kieran; their fathers, Gerald Robinson and Orlando Mendoza; Orlando's fiancée, Josephine Fortune; and their siblings, Rachel and Matteo; Zoe and Joaquin; and Cisco and his wife Delaney. Rachel and Zoe were in on the ruse, but his brothers and Delaney weren't and they believed they were witnessing a romance unfolding right before their eyes.

As they had waited to board the small chartered bus that would take them to the winery, Dana's friend Monica had flirted with him. But then Olivia had walked up and draped her arms around his neck and greeted him with a kiss that made his eyeballs roll back into his head. After that, Monica had kept her distance.

Normally, he would have been enticed by the challenge of a beautiful woman's reserve—especially one who had shown interest in him. After all, it was the thrill of the chase, and it was one of his favorite games. But not only did Monica virtually disappear, his attention kept drifting back to Olivia, who was seated beside him on the bus.

He admired the way her long dark hair was swept back from her face, accentuating dark, soulful eyes, high cheekbones and full lips that begged him to kiss them again. His eyes followed the graceful slope of her neck to the place where her blouse ended in a vee at her breastbone and just a hint of cleavage winked at him. She looked sleek and polished in her snug-fitting beige pants and black tank.

She leaned in toward him. "Thanks for doing this."

Her voice was quiet and husky and made him think of sex, even though he wasn't sure if she was expressing gratitude for the wine tasting trip or for going along with the ruse to draw her sister out of her pre-wedding funk.

"My pleasure." He watched her intently, realizing that in its own way this game of subterfuge was at once erotic and frustrating as hell. The two of them acted like they couldn't keep their hands off each other, like they were merely tolerating the others until they could finally sneak off to finish what they'd started.

Every single person here, with the exception of Rachel and Zoe, thought Olivia and he were sleeping together. The thought made his groin tighten even though the exact opposite was true. They were like the old back-lot Hollywood sets that looked real from the outside, but behind the scenes it was just prefabricated plywood braces and empty promises.

Even though he really could've used a cooldown, he put his hand on the back of her neck and caressed it. The gesture made her look up at him and when she did, he lowered his mouth to hers and planted a gentle kiss on her lips.

"Get a room, you two." Sophie laughed. Olivia had strategically chosen the seats in front of Sophie and Mason to give her sister a front-row seat for the show.

They ended the kiss and feigned embarrassment as Sophie leaned forward and braced her forearms on the seatback.

"So, my big sister isn't immune to love after all."

Her voice floated between them on a note of wonder. "You know, Alejandro, I called this relationship even before the two of you realized you were perfect for each other."

"Yes, you did, Sophie," Olivia said to her sister. She placed her hand on his leg and traced slow circles and she continued to gaze at Alejandro, as if she was so deeply in love she couldn't bear to look away. "You nailed it. You did."

Alejandro smiled. "What do you mean you called it?"

"That night at the Driskill bar," Sophie explained, "I said to Olivia that the two of you were perfect for each other. Not just because you're the last single Mendoza brother and she's the last single Fortune Robinson sister, but because you're perfect together. You're made for each other."

"We are perfect for each other," Alejandro echoed as he gazed at Olivia.

"Well, it's true," Sophie said. "You are the only person in the world that could make my sister believe in love. You're like King Arthur of Camelot, the only one who could pull Excalibur out of the stone."

He raised an eyebrow at Olivia. Had she really never been in love? What was it that would cause her to take such a hardline stance? What would make her close herself off? Granted, love was a risky endeavor. The heart was uncertain by nature. He'd learned that firsthand after he'd lost Anna.

"See, Olivia? I told you that there was someone for you. I told you that Alejandro was your man."

"Yes, you did, Sophie."

Something flickered in Olivia's gaze. She blinked and looked away. But it felt more like she was pulling away. Maybe she was performing the same reality check Alejandro himself was right now. Despite the hot kissing, tender touching and cozy embracing, it was all for show. Every bit of it. He needed to remind himself of that now and again. Hell, if he knew what was good for him, he would write a stern reminder on a figurative sign and nail it to the forefront of his mind. Because he could already see it would be very tempting to lose himself in this game.

Olivia scooted away from him and turned around in her seat to talk to her sister.

"I'm glad to see you're feeling better." Her voice was low. "You had us all worried for a while."

Alejandro didn't turn around. Instead, he sat facing forward and he caught his father, who was seated at the front of the bus, slanting a glance over his shoulder in Alejandro's direction. When the older man realized Alejandro had caught him looking, he pretended to be shifting so that he could more easily drop his arm around Josephine's shoulder. But Alejandro hadn't missed the curious look in his dad's eyes.

He pondered the vague conundrum of what he was going to say to his father and Josephine once they had a chance to corner him. Orlando was bound to be full of questions, and rightfully so. He was his father, after all. A father who wanted nothing more than for all of his children to be as happy as he was.

There was a long stretch of time after Alejandro's mother, Luz, died when he thought his father might never be happy again. Orlando had been so deeply in love with Luz that Alejandro and his siblings had feared that he might will himself into an early grave. That was so unlike the man who had always been so full of life.

When Luz died five years ago, Orlando had been bereft. Alejandro and his siblings had convinced him that he needed a change of scenery, that he needed to leave a lifetime of memories and the hustle and bustle of Miami for the more laidback pace of Horseback Hollow, Texas. That was when he met Josephine Fortune. Since then, Orlando had been like a new man.

Alejandro hated to lie to his dad. They'd always had a great relationship, but he'd promised Olivia he wouldn't tell anyone what they were up to. They couldn't risk anyone slipping up and tipping off Sophie. The more people who knew about the ruse, the greater the chance of someone spilling the beans.

Orlando was nothing if not understanding. As soon as the week was over and Sophie was happily off on her honeymoon, he would level with his dad. Orlando would understand.

Gerald Robinson, however, might be another matter.

Olivia's father sat in the front seat across the aisle from Orlando and Josephine. He'd arrived only moments before the bus left so Alejandro hadn't had an opportunity to introduce himself again. They'd met at his brothers' weddings, but it had only been in passing.

Alejandro ignored the dread that reminded him that Gerald Robinson would probably wonder about this sudden relationship. Any father with a daughter like Olivia would be protective.

He'd done a fair amount of research on Gerald Robinson the mogul, the genius businessman. The guy was formidable. He had a reputation for ruthlessly eliminating competition and systematically taking down his opponents.

Alejandro blinked away a sudden vision of Gerald enlisting his henchmen to teach him a lesson about messing with his daughter. But then he dismissed the thought because he wasn't messing with Olivia. He was helping her. Actually, he clarified to himself, he was messing around with Olivia to help Sophie.

This could get complicated in ways that he hadn't even thought of before he'd agreed to this farce.

Alejandro's hand instinctively found the tattoo on his forearm. He covered it with his palm, as if touching Anna's name might provide answers. The tattoo was his touchstone, anchoring him in the past and grounding him in the present all at once. It was a reminder that he'd been fortunate enough to know true love once. Not everyone was lucky like that. Olivia didn't even believe in love. He didn't know if it was because she'd been hurt so badly that it had cauterized her heart.

He glanced at her as she and her sister had their heads together, whispering and laughing, making happy sounds that had him convinced that their Saturday-night fight, the one that had nearly turned Sophie into a runaway bride, was not only a thing of the past—it was erased from the annals of their sister history.

The bus rounded the corner, bringing Hummingbird Ridge Vineyard into view with its inviting lodge and its acres of weathered grapevines standing like rows of stooped and gnarled old men waiting for the rapture.

The midday sun beat down, casting a golden light on the scene, making it one of the most beautiful sights Alejandro had ever seen.

The blood rushed in his ears as his pulse picked up at the thought of how hard he'd worked to bring his plans to life. Soon, this would all be his. His kingdom.

"Is that Hummingbird Ridge?" Olivia asked.

He nodded.

"It's beautiful," Olivia said. "It looks like a postcard. Isn't it sad that for as long as I've lived in Austin, I've never been to a Hill Country winery? So this is a real treat for so many reasons."

"Never?" Alejandro asked. "Why not?"

"That's a good question. I have no idea why not and I don't really have any good excuses. I guess I just haven't had time to venture out here. Or, actually, I've been so bogged down by the day-to-day grind that I haven't made time."

He wanted to ask her what she did for fun, if she even had fun. Or was she always all work and no play?

He wanted to tell her that he could help her with that, if she'd let him. After all, he had made an art form out of having fun while working his way to success. But the bus was pulling into the winery's parking lot. He made a mental note—right across the large sign in the forefront of his mind that reminded him their escapades were all for show—to help Olivia learn how to have fun this week. Right now, he had a winery to show off and a captive audience that was eager to learn more.

As the driver parked, Alejandro told her, "I'm going to go inside to make sure everything is ready for us. Will you corral everyone outside until I get back?"

"You bet."

She already had her work face on, ready to take charge. It would be fun to see her spring into action organizing everyone.

"Thanks. Why don't you take them for a walk around the grounds? There's a sculpture garden around the back. I want to make sure everyone gets a chance to enjoy it. I'll come and get you as soon as they're ready for us."

Without even thinking about it, he leaned in and kissed her. It felt natural. Maybe a little too natural. But she kissed him back. When she pulled away, they both seemed to have the same question in their eyes: *Is this okay?* And the same answer: *It's fine.*

He stood and made his way to the front of the bus. Since it was a weekday the staff had agreed to close the tasting room for their private party. A sign was

tacked to the large rough-hewn wooden door. It read:
"Closed for private party from 1pm-3pm. Please come
again." Alejandro reached out and grabbed the brass
handle and pulled the door. It creaked open, exposing
an airy reception area with high vaulted ceilings with
dark beams. A marble-topped tasting bar crowded
with wineglasses and corked bottles graced the wall
directly across from the front door. In the center of
the room, someone had set a wooden trestle table for
the tasting. They'd laid it with breads and cheeses
and other appetizers to pair with the various wines.

The rusty squeak of the door sounded behind Alejandro and he turned to see Gerald Robinson walk in.
The man stopped just inside the threshold, scowled
and took his time looking around, taking in everything as if he were judging the place and finding it
wanting. Even after his gaze skewered Alejandro,
Gerald didn't speak. He stood there silently, challenging him with his blank expression.

There he was—*the* Gerald Robinson. Creator of
empires, eviscerator of men who got in his way…
And of men who dated his daughter?

Obviously his brothers and Mason had battled the
monster and lived to marry his daughters.

When Gerald agreed to join them today, Alejandro
had known the mogul was bound to have a conversation with him about what Alejandro was doing with
Olivia. What the hell was he supposed to say? Lying
to Orlando was one thing—it wasn't really lying because he would confide the truth later—but lying
to Gerald by saying he was in love with his daugh-

ter was another. It was best to be proactive and take charge of the conversation.

"Mr. Robinson, welcome." Alejandro walked over to Olivia's father and extended his hand. "I'm Alejandro Mendoza. We've met before at Rachel's and Zoe's weddings."

Gerald offered a perfunctory shake, but his grip was firm and commanding. "I know who you are. Olivia tells me you're buying this place?"

"I am."

Again, Gerald's steely gaze pinned him to the spot. Alejandro steeled himself for the inevitable interrogation.

"Nice place," Gerald said. Unsmiling, he broke eye contact and gave the room another once-over. "You're from Miami. I take it you know something about wine."

They weren't questions. They were statements that proved the guy had already done some investigating. Hell, for all Alejandro knew the man might've hired a private detective to perform a full-scale inquiry.

It was fine if he had. Alejandro had nothing to hide. He made his living honestly.

"I know a lot about wine. Are you an oenophile?"

"I have no idea what you're talking about," Robinson said.

"An oenophile is a wine enthusiast," Alejandro explained.

Gerald scowled at him. "Why didn't you say that in the first place?"

It was a fair question. Gerald probably thought he

was being pretentious, showing off. Maybe he was. But that wasn't something he'd admit out loud.

"I don't like wine," Gerald said. "But I read something just the other day about how over the past few decades, Hill Country wineries have been growing steadily and Texas wine production has become a viable player in the industry. Fascinating. The article said that winemakers are forgoing the Napa Valley because it's expensive and exclusive and basically out of their reach."

That was exactly why Alejandro had chosen to buy a place in Texas. When he'd discovered it was a viable option it had almost seemed meant to be, since most of his immediate family had relocated to the Lone Star State. In fact, if he'd believed in fate, he might have thought it'd had a hand in aligning the stars and moon to make this possible. It just seemed to make sense that this was where he would invest the money his mother, Luz, had left him when she passed away.

In typical Luz fashion, she'd made arrangements to take care of her children even after she'd left this earth. She'd taken out a small life insurance policy, leaving equal sums to each of her five kids. She'd left each of them a handwritten note telling them how much she loved them, that it had been a privilege to be their mother and that she hoped the money she was leaving each of them would help make their dreams come true.

Alejandro had invested the gift from his mother and, while it wasn't enough to allow him to buy Hummingbird Ridge free and clear, that investment, along with the money he'd saved, was the seed money he needed to interest his cousins, Rodrigo and Stefan, and a couple of investors who would be silent partners. Together they had the buying power to make the deal. They were almost there. The last hurdle was to clear due diligence and inspections and they'd be home free.

"That's exactly why I chose Texas," Alejandro said. "Most of my family has relocated to Texas. I've had my eye on wineries here. I've made several scouting trips, during which I became friendly with Jack and Margaret Daily—the couple that owns Hummingbird Ridge. They wanted to sell and I wanted to buy. It just seemed like a good fit."

Gerald grunted as he stood there with his arms crossed. Alejandro couldn't tell if he was boring him or if the sound indicated contemplative interest.

"Hummingbird Ridge has been in Margaret's family for several generations," Alejandro explained. "She inherited it and wanted to pass it on to their daughter, but the daughter's not interested. She's a surgeon and doesn't have the time or the inclination to take over the family business. I asked them if they wanted to adopt me, but they said they'd cut me a deal instead," he joked, but Gerald didn't laugh.

"If I would've known it was for sale, I would've bought it."

"Really?" This was unexpected coming from a guy who professed to not like wine. "You're interested in getting involved in the wine industry?"

Gerald shrugged. "To diversify."

"If you find a vineyard and you do decide to invest, make sure you've got a good crew. Even though this is becoming one of the top wine production states, it still has its challenges. It has distinct regions that are different enough to the point of being incompatible in terms of vine selection. Depending on the area, the microclimatic and geographic factors can vary considerably, but that's what I find so appealing about it."

Gerald didn't say anything. Alejandro could tell from the man's body language that it was time to stop talking. So he just stood there. The faint whir of the air conditioner was the only sound in the room.

"Well," Gerald finally said, "thanks for arranging this tasting. And if you hurt my daughter, you'll answer to me and there will be hell to pay."

The older man's forced smile reminded Alejandro of a great white shark as Gerald turned around and let himself out of the tasting room.

"Alejandro, welcome. We're excited that you could be here today."

Alejandro turned to see Margaret stepping out of the office, which was located down a hallway to the right of the wine bar.

"Hi, Margaret. Everything looks great. Thanks for going the extra mile to make today special for my guests."

"My pleasure. Will they be arriving soon?"

"They're already here." He motioned to the door. "They're enjoying the grounds until you're ready for them."

"We're ready when you are," Margaret said. "Shall we invite them in?"

As Alejandro and Margaret set off to find the party, she told him that Jack was sorry to miss him, but he had some business in Dallas he had to take care of.

Alejandro's phone rang, interrupting the conversation. His cousin Stefan's name flashed on the screen. "Excuse me, Margaret. I need to take this call."

"That's fine, honey. I'll find everyone and bring them inside."

"Stefan, my man," Alejandro said. "You must have been picking up the good vibe. I'm standing here in the Hummingbird Ridge tasting room. What's going on?"

Stefan didn't speak right away and for a moment Alejandro thought they'd lost the connection.

"Stef, are you there?"

"I am. I don't have good news. Masterson is pulling out of the Hummingbird Ridge deal."

Alejandro's gut contracted. "Bad joke, bro."

"I wish it was a joke. It's not. We're not going to have the money we need to buy the place. We're going to be short by a third."

Chapter Six

That evening, Alejandro stared straight ahead at the stretch of highway ahead of him as he drove Olivia to the barbecue, which was hosted by Mason's family. Losing the investor was nothing more than a setback.

Still, if he'd had a shred of a hint that the deal wouldn't go through, he wouldn't have brought everyone to the winery. He would've come up with some other way to celebrate the brides and grooms, but he certainly wouldn't have dragged everyone out in the middle of all the wedding festivities had he known that the vineyard might not be his. Or at least he wouldn't have announced that it was his new venture. But after the sting of the setback had subsided a bit, his mind turned to more constructive thoughts: getting replacement funds.

Before they'd boarded the bus to leave for Austin, he'd asked Gerald Robinson if he could meet with him on Monday morning after the wedding because he wanted to present an investment opportunity in Hummingbird Ridge. It was a long shot, but Robinson hadn't cut him off at the knees. Instead, he'd dug around in his wallet and come up with a business card.

"Call my assistant and tell her I told you to set up a meeting." He hadn't asked any questions or expressed any interest; he'd just walked away and gotten on the bus.

Immediately, Alejandro had excused himself and had gone back inside the winery and placed the call. Before the bus had left Hummingbird Ridge, he had an appointment with Robinson on the books at three o'clock Monday afternoon. He'd have to change his flight back to Miami from Monday to Tuesday, but it was a small price to pay for possibly saving the winery purchase.

The biggest problem was whether or not to tell Olivia he was meeting with her father.

He remembered what she'd said about the guys who had used her to get to Gerald. He didn't want her to get the wrong idea, that he was using her. Sure, they weren't dating, but after weighing it, he thought it was best not to involve her so that she wouldn't feel obligated.

He kept hearing her say, *I owe you. I'll make it up to you*, after he'd agreed to help her with her plan to make Sophie think Olivia believed in love.

He didn't want her to feel beholden. Plus, he really didn't want to get into the details of how the deal was hanging by a thread. Not when it came to a business deal of this magnitude. If Gerald said no, that would be the end of it. She'd never know. If he said yes, he would tell Olivia.

"Do you want to talk about whatever is on your mind?" Olivia asked from beside him in his car.

He slanted a glance at her, but returned his focus to the road.

He had worked damn hard to keep his poker face in place. He hadn't wanted to spoil the festivities. Obviously he hadn't been as good at hiding his frustration as he'd intended. "Talk about what?"

"What's had you tied up in knots since the start of the tasting."

"I got a phone call while we were at the vineyard. There's a slight snag with one of the investors. But it's not a problem. Everything will be fine."

Telling her that much made him feel better. Since she'd picked up on his mood, sharing that was more honest than if he'd tried to pretend that nothing was wrong.

He deflected the focus off himself with his next comment. "And speaking of fine, it seems like Sophie and Mason are doing well. It's nice to see that your plan worked. I guess we make a convincing match."

On Friday evening, the wedding rehearsal went off without a hitch and Sophie seemed to be herself again, in full bride-to-be mode. Now she was seated across the rehearsal dinner table from Olivia, laughing and flirting with Mason, stealing kisses and whispering private words in his ear.

Good. The plan had worked out exactly as Olivia had hoped it would. In less than twenty-four hours Sophie and Mason would be on their honeymoon and Olivia would officially be disqualified from receiving the title Prewedding Homewrecker of the Year.

Maybe Sophie had simply experienced a case of cold feet, but Olivia still owned the responsibility of pushing her sister into the desperate weeds of despair after she brought up their parents' dismal excuse of a marriage. Ever since the night of the Fuzzy Handcuffs, Olivia had limited herself to one alcoholic beverage during wedding festivities—at the winery she had only allowed herself a single sip of each wine they had sampled. It was at once her own self-enforced punishment for being so sloppy at the bachelorette weekend and insurance that it wouldn't happen again.

Being one of the few sober people at the parties was a strange experience. But it was necessary. She could enjoy herself without social lubrication, and it was the only way to ensure that her sister actually made it down the aisle, headed in the right direction for the start of the rest of her life.

The private dining room where the rehearsal dinner was taking place was awash in golden candlelight and gorgeous white flowers. The party planner had strung hundreds of tiny golden twinkle lights around the room. She had crafted them into hanging topiaries and stuffed them into glass cylinders that were grouped with dozens of candles and more flowers to create ethereal tablescapes. It was a dinner fit for a princess—two princesses, Sophie and Dana. Olivia almost allowed herself to breathe a silent sigh of relief—almost—but she'd hold off on that until Sophie and Mason had been pronounced man and wife.

Still, she had never seen her little sister look so happy, and she couldn't help but smile along with her. But then she realized that as soon as Sophie and Mason said *I do*, she and Alejandro would part ways.

She slanted a glance at him and remembered the kiss at the luau. How it had started as a means to an end and had turned into something electrifying. His hands on her body. The way her body had responded to his touch, and how neither of them had seemed to want to stop. But they had. And now that it appeared certain that Sophie would make it down the aisle tomorrow evening, Olivia needed to start mentally distancing herself from Alejandro. She was going to miss him and his kiss. Miami was a long way from Austin. Not that either of them wanted to try to keep this chemistry alive long distance. Because chemistry did not a relationship make.

Even so, too bad he didn't live in Austin. If he had, maybe they could see if this chemistry could evolve into something less ethereal. But he didn't live in Austin and that's why it was safe for her to daydream about what-ifs that would never happen.

Although if he did end up buying that vineyard, he would be in Austin now and again. She thought about the way he'd looked when he'd told her about the snag with the investor. It had been obvious that he hadn't wanted to talk about it. That's why she hadn't pressed him further. Since she didn't want to pry, she had no idea where his financing stood. Even though she shouldn't get involved, she had an idea about how she might be able to help him—just in case he needed it. After all, she owed him. If not for him, Sophie might not have gone through with the wedding. Olivia felt like the least she could do was help Alejandro find a replacement investor. Her gaze combed the crowd until it landed on her father.

Yes, she just might be able to secure Alejandro's vineyard purchase. She would talk to her dad after the brides and grooms had each said *I do* and the wedding was over.

In the meantime, she was going to make sure she played her role of Cupid-struck lover to the hilt, to make sure Sophie didn't have any reason to back out at the last moment.

Matteo, Mason and Joaquin were talking about the eighteen holes they'd played that morning. Alejandro had begged off on the round of golf because he'd needed to make some phone calls.

The guys talked about bogeys and birdies and the difficulty of the fifteenth hole, but Olivia wasn't a golfer and the conversation didn't hold her interest. Alejandro seemed to be in his own world, too. She wondered where that world might be and who he might be thinking about.

Olivia leaned over so that her arm rested flush

against Alejandro's. She let her hand fall onto his thigh. Granted, his leg was hidden by the table and no one could see it, but it helped her get into character.

Following suit, Alejandro did the same thing, letting his hand wander over to her thigh. It happened so naturally. His thumb and forefinger toyed with the hem of her dress. The feel of his thumb on her bare leg sent shivers coiling outward from her belly.

In response, she traced tiny circles over his pant leg, on the inside of his thigh, going high, but not *too* high. This was for their own entertainment, of course, but it was just for play. He was teasing her and he was blurring the line between pretend romance and giving in to the attraction that they were both feeling. Last night's kiss had confirmed that. It had been filled with curiosity and longing and pent-up desire.

For a crazy moment she wondered what would happen if they just gave in to their feelings...

She thought it through, making a crazy attempt at justification. By making love with Alejandro, this act they had been putting on for Sophie's benefit wouldn't be a complete farce. It wouldn't be a total lie. Of course they wouldn't be in love as they claimed, but they would be involved. Even if she'd made love with Alejandro, they would still break up right on schedule and move on with their lives.

But in the end, common sense won because the thought of rendering herself so vulnerable to Alejandro, making love to him knowing that they would say goodbye, made her heart ache.

She laced her fingers through his and took his

hand off her leg, putting it on the table, where everyone could see.

This was just another act in the play. A play that was for her sister's benefit.

"May I have your attention, please," said Gerald Robinson. The room quieted down at the sound of her father's commanding voice. "Sophie and Mason, Dana and Kieran, please come up here. Join me. I'd like to say a few words. Even though the Montgomerys are cohosting this evening with me, I hope they won't mind me proposing a toast to the four kids whose lives will change forever tomorrow night."

Olivia flinched, suddenly wishing she could muzzle her father, because he was a man who spoke his mind and she could never be sure exactly what was going through that head of his. She squeezed Alejandro's hand as she watched the foursome join him at the front of the room.

"You okay?" he said, looking at her with eyes so dark and soulful it made Olivia's breath hitch.

"I'm fine. Or at least I hope I will be—or everything will be—" She gave an almost imperceptible nod toward her father and leaned in closer to whisper to Alejandro. He smelled good—like citrus and something grassy and clean. It instantly calmed her nerves. "I hope he doesn't decide to unload his ideas about love and marriage. I did that and we saw where that got us."

Alejandro smiled that lazy, hypnotizing smile of his. For a split second Olivia wanted to lean in and kiss him.

"If he does," Alejandro whispered, "we will just have to put in some overtime."

His gaze dropped to her lips and lingered for a moment before he freed his hand from hers and put his arm around her shoulder, pulling her close in a display so convincing that Olivia wanted to believe it was real.

Good grief. What the hell is wrong with me?

She inhaled, trying to clear her mind, but all she managed to accomplish was filling her senses with the scent of him. She needed to get some air.

Her father was in the middle of giving his toast. He hadn't said anything offensive yet—then again, Olivia had only been listening with half an ear—but there was still time.

She sat forward in her seat. "Will you excuse me for a moment, please?"

As she stood, she caught Zoe's eye.

Out in the hall both Rachel and Zoe fell into step with her as she made her way toward the ladies' bathroom.

The restroom was decorated with dainty pink flowered wallpaper and gold fixtures. It was divided into two sections: a sitting area with a love seat and a vanity where guests could freshen up makeup or wait for friends to finish in the second area, which contained the toilets and lavatories. The two areas were separated by old-fashioned swinging doors.

"What's going on?" Zoe said, once they were inside the restroom.

Olivia considered making a sarcastic quip about

being in here because nature called, but she was tired of pretending. That wasn't why she was here.

"For a moment, I was afraid our father was going to single-handedly undo all the hard work we've accomplished this week bringing Sophie and Mason back together. It's one thing for Sophie to get upset over my indiscretion—that's fixable, as evidenced by the events of this week. But if Dad is in one of his moods and he starts going to town and giving a dissertation on his views of the institution of marriage, I don't know if I'll be able to fix it."

"You can't worry about that," said Rachel. "She seems fine. I really doubt anything could sway her now. She loves Mason. I think if she did have another episode like she had last weekend, maybe it would be a good idea to question whether or not she was ready to get married."

"You're right," Olivia said. "It's just that we've come this far. I don't want anything to go wrong."

"I have something sticky on my fingers," Rachel said. "Come in here so I can wash my hands." She pushed through the double doors into the area with the sinks and stalls. Olivia and Zoe followed her.

"You are still blaming yourself and you need to stop," said Zoe. "You have done everything you can to ensure that Sophie makes it down the aisle. I mean, not many sisters would go to the lengths that you've gone to, pretending to be in love—although getting to cozy up to Alejandro Mendoza isn't really a hardship."

Rachel and Zoe laughed.

"I must admit you two have put on a pretty convincing performance this week," Zoe said. "There were times that even I believed you. I don't think anyone suspects that your relationship is anything but real. Certainly not Sophie. She'll be fine."

Rachel turned off the water and reached for a paper towel just as Sophie pushed through the double doors. Her smile was gone and so was her rosy glow. "So it was all an act? You and Alejandro have only been pretending to be in love with each other?"

Olivia's heart stopped. Rachel and Zoe stood frozen in place with huge eyes and gaping mouths.

"You lied to me." Sophie's voice was laced with hysteria and kept getting higher with each word. "Why would you do something like that, Olivia?"

Alejandro looked up at the feel of someone tapping him on the shoulder.

Rachel leaned down and whispered, "We have a situation. Can you help me, please?"

A feeling of dread spread over him as he glanced around the ballroom and realized that the other three Fortune Robinson sisters weren't in the room. He had no idea what was up. Had Sophie changed her mind again? She had looked perfectly happy a few moments ago when she had joined her father at the front of the room for the toast. Gerald Robinson had seemed uncharacteristically sentimental and Sophie had seemed to bubble over as she leaned in and kissed her father on the cheek. But Alejandro was quickly learning that the Fortune Robinson family was strangely complex. Just when he thought he had them figured out they left him guessing.

He followed Rachel to another room near the one where the rehearsal dinner was taking place and found Sophie reading Olivia the riot act.

"So this was all a horrible trick?" she asked.

"Sophie, I can explain if you'll just let me," Olivia said. She reached out to take hold of Sophie's hand, but Sophie pulled away.

"Don't. Don't touch me."

"Sophie, I did this for you. You were getting ready to make the biggest mistake of your life deciding not to marry Mason, and I felt like I'd caused it. I wanted to fix it. There's no reason for you to be mad—"

"No reason to be mad? You lied to me, Olivia. I suppose this has all been one big joke to you?"

"Calm down, Sophie," Zoe said. "You're acting like she stole your fiancé rather than try to help you make things right."

It seemed like Zoe's words didn't even register with Sophie.

"How many other people are in on this joke?" Sophie demanded. "How many? Tell me."

Olivia seemed to be stalling and stammering as Alejandro approached. She looked at him with desperation in her eyes, but she finally found her voice. "Only Zoe, Rachel and—"

"There you are, *querida*," Alejandro said. "I've been looking all over for you, my love. Is everything okay?"

"You can drop the act, Alejandro," Sophie said. "I know all about your little game and I don't appreciate it one bit."

"Game?" Alejandro asked, lacing his right fingers through Olivia's and putting a protective arm around her shoulder. "I have no idea what you're talking about."

Sophie wasn't buying it. "This." She gestured at Olivia and Alejandro with a dismissive wave of her hand. "This lovey-dovey act. Olivia isn't in love with you. She doesn't even believe in love. She's made that perfectly clear too many times over the years. So just stop. Right now. Okay? This is insulting."

Olivia glanced up at him with a look that suggested she wished she could melt into the ground. He did his best to reassure her with his eyes. *Don't worry. I've got this.*

He dropped his arm from Olivia's shoulder and pulled his fingers from her grasp. "Wow. Did I read this all wrong? I'm so embarrassed. I think we need to talk, because obviously I've gotten the wrong message."

Sophie snorted. "Please don't tell me she used you. She concocted this elaborate scheme and didn't even clue you in? Olivia?"

"No," Alejandro said. "I know it started out as a way to convince you, Sophie, that love was real. Olivia thought that the best way to do that was to make you think she had fallen in love with me. The funny thing is, somewhere along the way in the midst of all this craziness, we really did fall in love. Or at least I did, and I thought she felt the same way."

He turned back to Olivia. "After everything we've shared. I... I just don't know how I could have been so wrong. I know you said you didn't want to tell your sisters about how things have changed between us because you didn't want to upstage the wedding. But all those kisses we shared felt so real. I'm in love with you, Olivia. Maybe we should leave and talk about this privately. I don't want to ruin your sister's night. However, I do need to know right now if this is just a game to you."

He was playing his part so convincingly that he almost believed himself. It wasn't hard. Olivia Fortune Robinson would be a very easy woman to love. But then something flashed in her eyes that made him get ahold of himself and he knew she understood what she needed to do.

"No, it's not a game. I love you, too," she replied.

Sophie exhaled impatiently. Her mouth was tight and her dark eyes glistened with tears. Alejandro half expected her to stomp her foot. But she didn't. She got right to the point.

"Just knock it off, you guys. This really is getting to be insulting. The more you lie the more furious it's making me."

Alejandro waited a beat, giving Olivia the opportunity to come clean. When she didn't, he knew it was up to him to pull out the big guns. So he did the only logical thing he could do: he fell down on one knee and took Olivia's hands in his.

Zoe, Rachel and Sophie gasped in unison.

"If you feel the same way I do," he said, his gaze fixed on Olivia, "if you love me as much as I love you, then, Olivia Fortune Robinson, will you be my wife?"

Chapter Seven

Two hours before the wedding, Olivia watched as the stylist pinned a stunning cathedral-length veil to Sophie's head. The salon was abuzz with late-day clients. Dana, Monica, Rachel and Zoe had already come and gone. Madison, the owner of the salon where Olivia and her sisters had been coming for years, had already worked her magic on the rest of the bridal party. Sophie was the last of the lot since placing her long veil proved a little tricky. Unfortunately, it did nothing to quell her curiosity.

"When is Alejandro getting you a ring?" She turned to look at Olivia. Her expression promised she wasn't going to let this go.

"I need you to sit still and face forward, please," said Madison.

"Sophie, are you five years old?" Olivia asked. "Quit looking at me and do what Madison needs you to do. Come on, the wedding is in two hours and we still need to get to the hotel so we can get dressed."

Olivia had appointed herself Sophie's handmaiden for the day. After everything that had happened, she was doing her best to make sure her sister made it down the aisle on time. In the meantime, she needed to distract Sophie from the details of last night's surprise engagement. *Surprise* being the key word. It was the last thing she had expected from Alejandro, but it had worked like a charm. Sophie's mood had turned on a dime. One minute she had been furious with her for the deception—and frankly, Olivia had been at a loss for what to do—and the next minute she had been crying tears of happiness for her sister whom she thought would never find love.

By the time she and Alejandro had left Sophie, she had seemed convinced. Today, not so much. She hadn't outwardly questioned the sudden proposal, but she was full of questions.

"Well, if you would just answer my question, I wouldn't have to keep moving my head to look at you," Sophie said. "If you would just tell me, I could close my eyes and relax. You don't want to be the cause of the bride's anxiety, do you?"

Olivia walked over and stood in front of Sophie, and leaned her hip on the vanity in front of the chair. "I don't know when he's going to get me a ring, Sophie. His proposal was as much of a surprise for me as it was for you. I—"

"Wait," said Madison, stopping midpin. "You're engaged? When she was talking about a ring, I didn't realize she meant an engagement ring. I didn't know you were even dating anyone, much less engaged. Oh, my gosh! Olivia! That's fabulous news. Congratulations! Have you set a date?"

Olivia cringed inwardly, but she dug deep, determined to keep up the happy, newly engaged charade. Really, all she wanted to do was change the subject. Last night, Sophie had been so upset. Even though Alejandro had shocked her with a fake proposal, in hindsight it really was just about the only thing that would've worked.

Alejandro had indeed saved the night, but it was a temporary fix.

Olivia couldn't help but feel that they had dug themselves in deeper and wonder how she was going to mend things with her sister when she and Alejandro called off the engagement. They had a couple of weeks before they would have to deal with that. It wouldn't be an issue until after everyone got home from their honeymoon. By that time Alejandro would be back in Miami and Olivia would be left with the task of announcing the broken engagement. But that seemed worlds away.

"Madison, today is Sophie and Dana's wedding day," she told the hairdresser. "I don't want to steal their thunder by putting the spotlight on me. So let's focus on them and I will give you all the details the next time I see you. Is that a deal?"

"Of course," Madison said, returning her focus to Sophie's veil.

"Hey," said Sophie. "Dana's gone to the hotel. I'm the only bride here and I say I want to talk about the engagement. Did you really not have any inkling? I mean, I'm so happy for you, but you guys met a week ago." She turned her head slightly to look at Madison. "Well, actually, they didn't just meet. They've seen each other at Zoe's and Rachel's weddings. Alejandro is the brother of their husbands. My sisters have a thing for Mendoza men, I guess. But I digress." She turned back to Olivia. "*Inkling.* Did you really not have an inkling this was going to happen?

"Come on, Soph," Olivia said. "I mean it. I don't want today to be about me. Let's keep the proposal on the down-low for the time being. Okay?"

Sophie shrugged. "I'm almost more excited about this news than I am to walk down the aisle."

"I'm going to pretend you didn't just say that," Olivia said.

Sophie rolled her eyes and turned her head away from her sister. Madison sighed and put both hands on either side of Sophie's face and gently moved the bride back into position.

"If you keep moving your head, I'm going to stick a bobby pin up your nose."

Sophie squinted at Madison. "How could you stick a bobby pin up my nose if I'm looking in the opposite direction?"

Madison cocked a brow. "Obviously you don't understand. If you don't sit still, I'm going to stick a bobby pin up your nose on purpose. To get your attention. I really don't want to do that to you on your wedding day. So, please?"

Sophie looked momentarily stunned, but sat up straight and faced the front, folding her hands primly in her lap. "Okay. I'm sorry."

Olivia chuckled to herself. Madison was one of the few people who could get away with saying something like that without making Sophie mad.

"You know, it might be a good thing that he hasn't gotten the ring yet," said Sophie. "That means you can pick out exactly what you want."

She held up her left hand. The two-carat diamond glistened in the overhead lights. "Mason proposed to me with the ring of my dreams. He knows me. He gets me. I am so lucky."

Sophie paused for a long moment and Olivia thought that they had turned a corner, until her sister said, "But don't worry, you and Alejandro will have the rest of your lives to get to know each other. I mean, on one level, I think you two know each other better than some couples who have been together for decades. That's what love at first sight is—or in your case, second or third sight." She smirked at her own joke, then went on, undeterred. "I think we need to announce your engagement tonight."

Olivia held up her hands. "No. Stop. Look, we have talked about nothing else but Alejandro and me since we've been here. That's precisely why I'm asking you to not say anything about our engagement tonight. No, scratch that. I'm asking you to not even *think* about my engagement tonight. I want you to focus on your own wedding. Soph, this is *your* night. I promise we can make the big announcement after you all return from your honeymoons. And not a minute sooner, okay?"

God help me.

Sophie shrugged. She looked like an angel in her lace veil. Her dark hair was pulled back away from her face, accentuating her exquisite cheekbones. The makeup artist had done a beautiful job creating a smoky eye that brought out the almond shape of Sophie's without looking too heavy. It was sweet and sultry… It was just right.

"When we get home from Tahiti," Sophie said, "Mason and I are going to throw the biggest, splashiest, most spectacular engagement party for you and Alejandro. We're going to invite everybody in Austin and Miami. Because it's a pretty spectacular happening when my sister, who had sworn for as far back as I can remember that she didn't believe in love, finally meets the man who makes a believer out of her. How does that sound?"

Sophie looked Olivia square in the eyes and held her gaze. Olivia did her best not to squirm.

Liar, liar. Pants on fire.

"That sounds—" Olivia's voice broke. She cleared her throat. "That sounds fabulous. But you might want to discuss the rather large guest list with Mason before you commit."

Still holding her sister's gaze, a slow Mona Lisa–like smile bloomed on Sophie's face.

"Mason will be happy to host the engagement party of the century for you and Alejandro. After all you've done for us."

Olivia couldn't breathe.

Oh, no. Oh, boy. Here we go.

She hoped she didn't look as pale as she felt.

"But you know," Sophie said, "it really was just a temporary case of cold feet. I would've married Mason no matter what. Because I love him and I can't imagine my life without him."

To Olivia's great relief, the double wedding went off without a hiccup. Sophie and Mason, Kieran and Dana were joined together as husband and wife in the grand ballroom of the Driskill Hotel, in front of nearly five hundred of their closest friends and family members.

The ballroom was festooned in white flowers—peonies, roses, lilies of the valley, freesias and hydrangeas arranged in tall gold-toned vases. The place looked like a florist's shop had exploded and it was glorious. The guests sat in gilded chairs situated in two sections on either side of an aisle. But tonight there weren't brides' and grooms' sides. The bridal couples had made it clear that everyone was gathered for the sake of love.

The place proved a perfect backdrop for her sister and sister-in-law.

Sophie looked stunning in her satin-and-lace ball gown, with its long train and veil trailing behind her. She looked like royalty.

Dana looked artistic and beautiful in the vintage silk shantung wedding gown that belonged to the grandmother of her maid of honor, Monica. She had graciously lent it to Dana for the special day and it served as both her something old and something borrowed. If Dana had designed a wedding gown for herself, it couldn't have been any more perfect than that one.

Honestly, Dana and Sophie both looked so radiant they could have worn bathrobes and slippers and still looked gorgeous. They were both so full of love as they promised to love, honor and respect their grooms for the rest of their lives.

As Olivia listened to the minister's touching opening words, her gaze picked Alejandro out of the guests. When he caught her looking at him, Olivia couldn't look away. Emotions she'd never experienced before zinged through her—happiness for the two couples pledging their love before God and everyone, wistfulness at the beauty of that love, and maybe even a touch of envy. She may not believe in love, but never in her entire life had she wished she did more than that moment.

Little Rosabelle, Dana and Kieran's adopted daughter, was the one who drew her out of her reverie. Bedecked in her pink princess dress, complete with floral crown, four-year-old Rosie was the flower girl. She did a fabulous job strewing rose petals down the aisle. Her new nanny, Elaine, stood at the side of the dais, smiling encouragingly at the little girl, poised at the ready to gently correct Rosie's course should she veer off track. But the child played her part perfectly, smiling bashfully at the guests seated on her either side. Given that she was so young and it was getting close to her bedtime, Rosie couldn't have done a better job.

At the beginning of the ceremony she stood with the bridal party. It was no surprise when she grew a little restless. Standing next to Olivia, she began to entertain herself by playing with the skirt of Olivia's dress. She grabbed a handful of skirt and pulled it around herself like a cape. It enlisted titters and *awwws* from the audience. The sound made Rosie hide her face and then peek out from the fabric. When she saw everyone looking at her, she stepped around behind Olivia and hid. Olivia placed a reassuring hand on the little girl's blond curls. Actually, she didn't blame her one bit for wanting to hide. She was getting a little weary of these wedding games herself. There were many times this week when she had wanted to hide her face from the world. But her sister was happy and within a matter of minutes she would be married. It was all worth it.

Alejandro was smiling at her again. He looked so handsome in his dark suit and white shirt. It was a different look from the cool Miami casual that he had projected most of the week. The more dressed-up look suited him. He was such a handsome man. All of his brothers were married. Why wasn't he?

Olivia recalled the conversation she and her sisters had last week at the bachelorette party before everything blew up. If she were inclined to be a ro-

mantic she might have believed that the reason Alejandro had never married was because he had been
waiting for her.

But that was just crazy.

"By the power vested in me," said the officiant,
"I now pronounce you husband and wife. Err—husbands and wives?" The man shrugged and looked out
at the guests. "Ladies and gentlemen, it is my pleasure to present to you Mr. and Mrs. Mason Montgomery and Mr. and Mrs. Kieran Fortune Robinson."

The guests erupted into boisterous applause as
the recessional music sounded, signaling the end of
the ceremony. Olivia handed Sophie her bouquet,
scooped up Rosie, balancing her on her hip as she
waited her turn to walk back down the aisle.

The bridal party exited the room where the ceremony had taken place and waited for the wedding
planners to usher everyone out and into the room
where they could enjoy cocktails and hors d'oeuvres.
Then the bridal party and immediate family returned
to the ceremony room for pictures.

They were using the same photographer as they'd
used for Rachel's and Zoe's weddings, because she
had done a beautiful job. But Olivia didn't remember
the photos taking this long.

Joaquin and Matteo Mendoza were in the pho-
tographs because they were married to her sisters
and therefore full-fledged immediate family. As with
Alejandro, they had not been in the bridal party, so
at first impulse it seemed strange that they would be

in the pictures and Alejandro wouldn't. But it made sense.

I think maybe Alejandro would be a perfect match for Olivia.

She tried to blink away the memory of her sister's words. It was just crazy girl talk.

Isn't it a coincidence that he's the last single Mendoza and you're the last single Fortune Robinson?

Obviously it was time for a reality check. There were good reasons that the two of them were still single. Good sense topped the list.

It had been a long week of wedding festivities and pretending. She was tired and her defenses were down. That always happened when she let herself get worn out. That was the only reason she was thinking these irrational thoughts as she watched her sisters interact with their husbands.

As the photographer arranged them into a grouping for a shot of the entire family Sophie stepped out of place and surveyed the group.

"Where is Alejandro?" she asked. "It's my party and I'll do what I want to," she said with a sassy smile. "And I want Alejandro in the family picture. It's important."

"It's not just your party," Olivia reminded her sister.

"Dana?" Sophie asked. "Do you mind if Alejandro is in the family picture?"

Dana shook her head. "Of course not. It's fine."

"Mason? Kieran?" Sophie said. "Any objections?"

As they indicated their approval, Sophie shot her sister a triumphant look.

Sophie wasn't letting this go. Olivia realized if she put up too much of a fight, things could get ugly. Granted, Sophie and Mason were married. Technically, her job was done. However, if she took this opportunity to announce that there was no engagement or that they had called off the engagement, pretending it was too sudden or logistically difficult, it would cast a dark cloud over the festivities.

This was one of those times when it was best to lose the battle so she could win the war. In that spirit, the best thing she could do was to just go along with it.

"In that case, if nobody objects I will go find Alejandro," Olivia said. "I'll be back as soon as I can."

It wasn't hard to locate him. He was standing with his father and Josephine, sipping a cocktail that looked like scotch and soda. He was holding a flute of champagne in the other hand. As she approached she was about to tease him about being a double-fisted drinker, but he smiled the warmest smile at her and held out the champagne.

"This is for you," he said. "You look like you could use it."

"I look that bad, huh?"

His smile faded. "No, not at all. It was just a figure of speech. You look beautiful."

Olivia felt her face warm at the sincere compliment. She never blushed. It was unfortunate that her body was choosing this moment to start. Then again, her body seemed to have a mind of its own when it came to Alejandro.

Just accept the compliment, she told herself. It was only a compliment. "Thank you. Hello, Orlando. Josephine, you look lovely. I'm so glad you both could be here for the wedding. It means a lot to our family."

They exchanged pleasantries about the ceremony and about how adorable Rosabelle was in her flower girl debut.

"You're so good with children," Josephine said. "Do you have any of your own?"

A hiccup of a laugh bubbled up in Olivia's throat. "Oh, heavens no. I'm not married. Of course, you know that since— I mean, I've never been married."

Her gaze fluttered to Alejandro, and she felt her face heat up again.

"I'm sorry to barge in but, Alejandro, your presence is requested in the photo room."

Photo room? Ugh. Get ahold of yourself.

"I mean, the bridal party would like for you to be in some of the pictures, if you don't mind."

She smiled and tried to look normal, but she felt like one of those grimacing emoticons.

"I don't mind at all," Alejandro said, just as calm and cool as if she had asked him to bring the car around so they could escape this circus.

Now, there was an idea. Maybe they should get in his rental car and just keep driving until they were far away from here. Maybe they could go to Miami. She could stay until both couples were back from their honeymoons, when she could announce that she and

Alejandro were no longer engaged. Then it wouldn't be a bombshell. In fact, Sophie might be so wrapped up in her own marital bliss that she wouldn't want the gray clouds of a broken engagement to shadow her own happiness.

"Where should we go?" Alejandro asked, waiting on her to lead him.

"Miami," Olivia mused aloud. "Let's go to Miami. Right now."

Alejandro shook his head and laughed. "That's one of the things I like the best about her," he said to his father and Josephine. "She has the best sense of humor. She always keeps me laughing and guessing."

The three of them laughed again and Olivia joined in so that they would believe that she really was just making a joke that hinted at her being a weary maid of honor.

If they only knew.

Actually, no. She didn't want them to know the truth. She didn't want anyone else to know about the ticking time bomb that she had created. She simply wanted to pacify her sister until the married couples got into their respective limousines and drove off into the night toward the first days of the rest of their lives.

She took his arm to lead him toward the photo room. After they had said their goodbyes to Josephine and Orlando and were out of earshot, Alejandro asked, "Why do they want me in the photos?"

Olivia slanted him a look that suggested he should know why. "Because, darling, you are my fiancé. Remember?"

"Right." He ran a palm over his eyes and raked his fingers through his hair, a tic that Olivia was beginning to associate with him being stressed. "Did Sophie tell everyone?"

Olivia shook her head. "No, but she is definitely testing me. I can't tell if she's on to us or if she's just excited because she thinks I've finally come over to the dark side."

"The dark side? Is that what you think of marriage?"

Maybe she was being overly sensitive, but there seemed to be a bit of rebuke in his tone.

"Don't you?" she answered. "I mean, you're not married and how old are you?"

"I'm thirty-four. And no, I don't necessarily think of marriage as the dark side."

"Then why aren't you married?" She instantly regretted asking the question that had been lurking in the back of her mind since she realized he was the last single Mendoza. "Or do weddings make you sentimental?"

He shot her a look. "I was actually engaged once."

The revelation hit Olivia like a sucker punch. "Really? What happened? I mean, if you don't mind me asking. I really thought you and I were similar in our thoughts about marriage."

One side of his mouth quirked up. "That's what happens when you assume."

She made a show of flinching. She remembered the old saying—*when you assume you make an ass out of u and me.* She arched a brow as she asked, "Are you calling me an ass, Alejandro?"

"Don't be ridiculous." The way he looked at her had her blushing, and inwardly going to pieces. It should be illegal for a man to look at a woman like he looked at her, making her feel things she shouldn't be feeling in this elaborate charade that they had orchestrated. Especially when he was set to leave in a couple of days.

"Again, when you assume, you run the risk of jumping to wrong conclusions," he said as he reached for the door to the ballroom where the ceremony had taken place. "Here we are, my most cherished fiancée." His dark eyes danced with mischief. "Let's give the bride the show she's expecting."

They were already inside the ballroom when Olivia realized how neatly Alejandro had evaded her question. He'd been engaged. Who was the woman he had loved enough to want to spend the rest of his life with—or at least want that for a brief period of time? What had happened to break up the engagement?

Now wasn't the time, but she fully intended to find out.

Alejandro's participation in the photos hadn't taken long. Sophie had only wanted him in one shot: the family photo. He had stood on the end and quietly joked with Olivia that they could cut him out of the picture if they wanted to. He probably should've found a way to gracefully bow out of the photo session. She could've told them she couldn't find him.

But it was done now. He was officially part of the family photo.

He got the distinct feeling that Sophie might've been calling their bluff by including him in the family shot. If she was, then she knew she was taking a chance. Maybe she'd had the photographer snap a few shots without him after he'd left.

This wasn't the first time he'd wondered if he'd pushed the envelope too far when he had proposed to Olivia in front of Sophie and her sisters. But seeing Olivia in distress had made him desperate to fix the situation. He'd just wanted to see her smile again. Of course, he wanted Sophie to be okay, too, but for a crazed moment, when he'd seen Olivia in such turmoil, he'd known he had to make things right. His knee-jerk reaction had been a proposal.

There was no getting around it now. The fake-proposal die was cast.

Before he returned to Miami, he would help Olivia clean up any family repercussions the "breakup" might cause. It was important they left family relations as good as possible. Olivia had already said she would be the heavy and take responsibility for the breakup. She'd claim they'd gotten swept away by the romance of the double wedding, but with distance and a fresh perspective, she realized she wasn't ready for a lifetime commitment.

Alejandro was prepared for the breakup. What he hadn't thought through was that he would have to delay his meeting to present the investment proposal to Gerald Robinson until after they called off the engagement. He didn't want it to appear that he was using Olivia for his own personal gain.

He'd debated whether or not to tell Olivia about his plan to ask her father to invest in Hummingbird Ridge. He'd ultimately come to the conclusion that it was best not to involve her. It was a long shot that he would buy in anyway.

If Robinson said no, Alejandro was perfectly prepared to leave it at that—no hard feelings. He didn't want Olivia to feel as if she needed to plead his case because she owed him.

Most people wouldn't feel the need to get involved on someone's behalf, but Olivia was different. Once she invested in someone, she was all in. Making sure her sister made it down the aisle was a case in point. She'd said more than once that she would make it up to him for helping her. A sixth sense told him that if she knew about the investor dropping out, she'd make it her mission to make that right. He couldn't take that chance. He'd fight his own fight.

If Gerald wasn't interested, he'd return to Miami and continue the frantic search for replacement funding. He could only hope that the Dailys wouldn't find another buyer before that. They had been so kind to refund his deposit, though they had every right to keep the money as stated in the contract. But Jack Daily had said he couldn't take the money in good conscience. That was one of the things that Alejandro loved about that winery in particular. It came from good stock, and he wasn't simply talking about the vines. He was talking about the family who had invested generations of blood, sweat and tears to make it what it was today.

They were good people and if he was given the chance, he wanted to carry on that legacy.

However, the way they'd left things was that if a viable buyer materialized before Alejandro could come up with the money, they would have to take the offer.

The Dailys were ready for the next phase in their life. They deserved the chance to write this next chapter. He hoped he would be able to write his own next chapter at Hummingbird Ridge. It would put him a hell of a lot closer to Austin than Miami. It would be easier to see Olivia if she was into seeing him. Maybe then he'd be able to figure out what had made her so down on marriage and romance.

The band leader called the crowd to order, putting an end to Alejandro's reverie. The man's deep baritone voice introduced the bridal party. As Olivia walked in, Alejandro watched her scan the crowd and find him.

He'd never met anyone who could flirt with her eyes the way Olivia did. She had great eyes. He felt mesmerized as she stood with the other bridesmaids and groomsmen until the brides and grooms had entered the room, acknowledged their guests and took to the parquet floor for their first dance.

She looked confident and happy—not a bit worried—as she closed the distance between them. If she wasn't worried, he wouldn't worry. At that moment, he decided he was going to forget all the challenges he was facing with the vineyard and the charade and just enjoy himself tonight. It was one of the easiest decisions he'd made in ages.

Olivia couldn't remember when she'd had so much fun at a wedding. It wasn't usually her preferred way to spend a Saturday night. But Alejandro knew how to show a girl a good time. The ballroom was awash in gold and white and there were so many flowers and tiny golden twinkling lights it seemed like their very own secret garden right in the middle of the busy city.

Sophie and Dana opted not to torture the bridal party by confining everyone to a head table. Instead, the two newly married couples dined together and the rest of the bridal party was dispersed among the guests. It was no surprise that they had seated Olivia and Alejandro together. If they hadn't, Olivia had been prepared to do some place card swapping—all for the sake of keeping up their charade, of course.

After dinner—a salad of warm goat cheese with gold and red baby beets; a surf and turf of filet mignon and sea bass served with truffle mushroom risotto—the dance floor heated up.

Alejandro was a good dancer. Olivia had no idea why she thought he might be reserved, but he wasn't at all. They danced to every song and by the time the band slowed things down with a ballad, it seemed perfectly natural when Alejandro, her fake fiancé, pulled her into his arms and held her close.

In the past, Olivia had always had a problem with slow dancing because most of the men she'd danced with had accused her of trying to lead. They would tell her to relax, to feel and respond to the subtle messages they sent with their bodies. Obviously either they were much too subtle—subtext: not man enough—with their bodily messages or she simply wasn't picking up their vibe.

Tonight, as she and Alejandro swayed to the music, was the first time she understood what it meant to let the man lead. Or maybe it was the first time she'd wanted to let someone else lead.

For the duration of the song, Olivia let herself imagine what it would be like if this pretend relationship was real. What would it be like to really be engaged to Alejandro Mendoza? She let herself go there, envisioning everything from what dress she would wear at their wedding—a mermaid-style gown that had caught her eye when she'd gone with Sophie for her final fitting—to what would happen on their honeymoon.

Ooooh, the honeymoon.

The thought made her breath catch. She closed her eyes as tiny points of warmth radiated out from her belly, making her lean into Alejandro and snuggle into his shoulder as they danced.

By the time the song ended, Olivia felt a little off-kilter. The two of them stepped apart, allowing a respectable amount of space between them. Sophie's voice broke the spell.

"I hope you all are having fun," she said. She was holding the lead singer's microphone with one hand. She had a champagne flute in the other. "Before the night gets away from me, I wanted to take this opportunity to give a shout-out to my sister, Olivia."

Olivia's heart leaped.

Oh, no. Please tell me she's not going to do what I think she's going to do.

Olivia grabbed Alejandro's arm to steady herself. He covered her hand with his left hand. She didn't dare look at him because she was trying to catch Sophie's eye to silently beg her not to do what it was becoming more and more apparent that she was about to do. But Sophie skillfully looked everywhere but at Olivia.

"My sister Olivia is my rock," Sophie said. "She's always thinking of and doing things for others. So often, she sacrifices her own needs for those she loves, and she doesn't get the credit she deserves. Olivia and Alejandro, I'm sorry for doubting you two. They know what I mean by that, so I won't bore you with the details. But I will say this—and my sister asked me not to say anything about this because she didn't want to steal my and Dana's thunder—because I just can't resist. Olivia and Alejandro have some great news."

She lifted her champagne flute and smiled broadly. "Everyone, please raise your glasses to the most recent Fortune Robinson bride-to-be and Mendoza groom-to-be. Olivia and Alejandro are engaged to be married."

Chapter Eight

After the wedding, as soon as the brides and grooms were off in a send-off shower of sweet-smelling lavender buds, Alejandro drove Olivia home to her condo in the Barton Hills neighborhood of Austin.

All she wanted was to get out of her bridesmaid dress and the pinching heels, take her hair down and get away from the flood of congratulations that had washed in after Sophie's little announcement.

They were both exhausted and contemplative, so they were mostly quiet in the car. They didn't talk about a plan, but Olivia knew they needed to before Alejandro left her place tonight.

As she changed into her heather gray yoga pants and a soft white T-shirt, she came up with a plan and was ready to present a strong case when she walked back into the living room. Alejandro was on the same page because he took the words right out of her mouth when he asked, "What are we going to do now?"

"First, I'm going to open a bottle of wine," she said. "That's what I'm going to do right now."

"Sounds good to me. Do you think that we're okay sticking to the original plan?"

She stopped on her way into the kitchen and looked back at him. "You mean breaking up tomorrow?"

He shrugged.

"I was hoping we could stay in character at least until after Sophie and Mason were home from their honeymoon and settled into married life. Does that work for you?"

"When will they be back?"

"They're only going away for a week. Mason has some business he needs to take care of. Then I think they're planning a longer trip in the fall."

He seemed to mull things over for a moment. "Yeah, I think I can make that work. I have some Hummingbird Ridge business, but nothing I can't tend to while I'm here."

"Great! A week should be long enough for the wedding sparkle to wear off and for us to realize we were swept away by the romance. Then we can 'take a break.'" She bracketed the words with air quotes. "I'm happy to be the heavy. I'll tell everyone I felt like things were just moving too fast. I'll confess that I got caught up in the romance of the wedding and while I think the world of you, I need time to think things over. My family won't be surprised, believe me. In fact, I'll bet they're already placing wagers on how long it will take me to call off the engagement."

Alejandro frowned at her. "I thought maybe your cynicism about love was all an act, but you've almost convinced me that you're really not a believer."

He was quiet for a moment, as if he was giving her the chance to tell him he was wrong, that it really was an act. When she didn't say anything, he asked, "What happened to sour you on love?"

Biting her lip, she looked away, toward the kitchen. Why did he care? She could read all sorts of things into that, but she wasn't going to.

"How about that glass of wine?" she asked, trying to buy herself a little more time. "After the day I've had, I'm going to need a glass of wine or two if we're going to have this conversation."

"Sure, thanks. That sounds good."

"Is red okay? I have white, but it's not cold."

"Red is perfect. May I help?"

She opened the cabinet and took down the wineglasses, hoping by avoiding the question he would get the hint that she didn't want to talk about it. "I'm good. I've got this."

The phrase was a pep talk for herself. Even though she didn't really want to talk about it, maybe she owed him a little insight about her parents' dynamics. After all, two Mendozas were part of the family and they were bound to pick up on the tension, if her sisters hadn't already filled them in. Alejandro had been so good to help her, and he did care enough to ask. He didn't strike her as the type who would dig just to be nosy. But why was he asking? What did that mean? She supposed it was possible for a man to care about a woman in a purely platonic way, although she had never had any successful relationships of that nature with men. And truth be told, if circumstances were different—if they weren't practically family—maybe she would want more than something platonic with Alejandro. But if it got messy… No, she'd better leave well enough alone.

"When are Dana and Kieran back?"

"They are going to be gone longer. They're heading to Paris for ten days," she said. "Did you meet Elaine Wagner tonight—the new nanny they'd hired to care for Rosabelle? She was the kid-wrangler tonight. She has a son who's just about Rosie's age. She's going to look after Rosie and her dog Sammy. You know that Dana and Kieran adopted Rosie after her father died, right?" She didn't wait for Alejandro's response before she continued.

"Having Elaine come on board has given Kieran and Dana enough peace of mind to know that they can get away for a while. After all they've been through—and with this whirlwind wedding—they deserve some time away."

She looked across the open-concept kitchen and saw Alejandro watching her intently. Since talking about Dana and Kieran had seemed to divert the conversation from her folks, she decided to continue.

"When they get back they're going to live at Dana's house. They want to get a new place together, but with the wedding put on the fast track and the honeymoon trip to Paris they haven't had a spare minute to begin the search. But Dana's house has a nice big yard for Rosabelle and Sammy to play in. Really, there's no need to rush the process. Everything will happen in good time."

She paused to pull the lever of the corkscrew and yank the cork out of the bottle. She knew she was rambling, but it seemed to have worked.

She set aside the cork from the wine, a Cabernet Sauvignon from the Columbia Valley, which *Wine Spectator* had scored a ninety-six. She wasn't a wine connoisseur, but she knew what she liked and she hoped this would be suitable for Alejandro. She poured the wine, secured both glasses between the fingers of her left hand, grabbed the bottle with her right and joined Alejandro in the living room. He was sitting on the couch, with one arm stretched out along the back. He looked so at home, like he belonged there.

As she set the wine bottle down on the coffee table, she realized she was nervous. Even so, she took a seat next to him on the couch rather than choosing the gray toile-print wingback chair. It reminded her of that first night in the Driskill bar when she'd moved from the chair to sit next to him. She hadn't been so drunk that she didn't remember it had felt so natural to sit next to him and just lean in and start kissing him. Of course, they'd kissed many times since. She wondered what he would do if she leaned in and kissed him right now.

She was tempted, but she didn't do it. Instead, she handed him a wineglass.

As had become their custom, they purposefully locked gazes before clinking their glasses. She thought about making another joke about good sex, but she just couldn't summon words that wouldn't sound rehashed or recycled, like ground they had already covered. Was that because she knew they were coming up on the final act of this performance?

With Sophie married and away on her honeymoon, did they really need to stay together? Wouldn't it be easier to end it now? Sophie was a big girl, and if Olivia was perfectly honest with herself she knew that Sophie had gone through with her marriage of her own volition. Olivia and Alejandro dating or not dating, being engaged or not, would not make one bit of difference in her sister's relationship.

If she knew what was best for both Alejandro and herself, she should tell him right now that it would be better for him to leave as planned. Funny though, she really wasn't ready for this to end. She'd gotten used to him being around. Even if it was a farce, she had gotten used to being part of a couple with him.

Alejandro and Olivia.

Olivia and Alejandro.

She liked the sound of that.

She traced the rim of her wineglass with her finger. Even after only a week it sounded natural to link their names. Would they remain friends and keep in touch after he went back to Miami? Would he make a point of ringing her up when he came to Texas on vineyard business? She hoped so. In fact, she wanted that very much.

She looked at him, mustering the will to tell him he was free to go if he needed to, but instead, what came out was "If we're going to make this engagement look convincing, don't you think you should check out of the Driskill and move in here with me?"

He looked surprised, as if he hadn't considered the possibility, and she braced herself for him to be the voice of reason, to not only decline but say everything she had been thinking only moments ago. That it was time to break up. Time to come clean. Time to move on.

"Are you sure?" he asked.

"Since short-term rentals are hard to come by and hotels are uncomfortable and expensive, you can move into one of the spare bedrooms in my condo," she said.

"Short-term rental?" His brows knit together. "I thought we were only talking about a week."

"Yes, well, I was just thinking that you might not want to pay for a hotel. Unless you want to, of course."

She cringed inwardly. This wasn't going the way she'd hoped. Maybe she should just make it easy on both of them and cut him loose.

"No. I see what you're saying and I appreciate it," he said. "I just don't want to impose. It's not easy having someone in your space, even for a week."

True. But it was definitely easier to host a guest

when you wanted the person there. And she didn't mind Alejandro being in her space.

"It'll be fine. And it'll appear more convincing if we're living together. It's the least I can do after all you've done to help me."

"It wasn't such a hardship," he said. For a moment, something shifted between them. She swore he was going to lean in and kiss her. But then she glanced down at her wineglass and when she looked back up the spell was broken.

"I will have to cook dinner for you while I'm here," he said. "It'll give me the chance to show off my culinary chops. I'm happy to say I know my way around the kitchen."

"Did you learn to cook so you could get the girls?"

He laughed. "Of course. Works every time."

She loved the way his eyes came to life when they bantered. Kissing him felt almost as natural as verbally sparring with him.

"How about this?" he said. "I'll earn my keep by cooking for you."

"Works for me. I've been told I have many talents, but domestic pursuits are not among them." She chuckled.

"Hey, my birthday is next week," she said. "Why don't you cook dinner for me then? Otherwise, my parents might insist on celebrating with us."

"Do you think so? I got the distinct feeling that your parents were avoiding me tonight after Sophie's announcement. I'd mentally prepared myself for what I would say to them, but it was probably for the best that they focused on your sister's and brother's wedding. If your dad is one of those old-fashioned types that gets offended if a guy doesn't ask for his daughter's hand, I didn't want to face the wrath of Gerald Robinson. That would've definitely been a party foul."

"You don't have anything to worry about. My father isn't really the traditional type when it comes to love and marriage. In fact, if you asked his permission to marry me, he would probably think you were up to something. Or at the very least sucking up."

"Have they said anything to you?" he asked.

"My mother cornered me earlier tonight. She said she was happy for us and she wants to get to know you better. She and my father want to take us out for dinner. Which means *she* wants to go out to dinner and my father probably knows nothing about it. She was trying to get us to come over tomorrow night, but I told her that we were both busy. I'll keep putting her off as long as I can. Especially for my birthday."

He picked up the bottle and refilled her wineglass. "What day is your birthday?"

"It's next Saturday."

"Maybe you should celebrate with them. When I was growing up, birthdays were always a big deal in our house. My mother would have a cake for us and we got to pick whatever we wanted for dinner."

Olivia shifted, and pulled one foot up and balanced it on her knee. She began to massage her foot. When she noticed him watching her hands, she said,

"Sorry, my feet hurt after standing in those heels all night."

"Here," he said, "put your feet in my lap. I give a mean foot massage."

She looked a little taken aback. For a moment he thought she was going to refuse, but she swung her legs up onto the couch and stretched out so that her feet were in his lap.

He used his thumb to draw small, firm circles on the ball of her foot.

She tilted her head back and moaned. It made him think of the night in the Driskill bar when she kissed him. He had a nearly overwhelming urge to lean over and see if her lips tasted as sweet as they had that night. But it probably wouldn't be a good move since he was going to be moving in with her and they needed to keep things cool just a little longer.

"That feels so good," she said. "Are you close to your parents? It sounds as if they made a big deal over making you feel special on your birthday."

"I'm close to my dad. My mom passed away about five years ago."

"I'm sorry."

He shrugged. "Thanks. My mom was a wonderful woman. We all took her loss pretty hard. But it's good to see my dad happy again with Josephine. There was a time when it seemed like he would never be the same again. I know you and your sisters are close but are you close to your folks? You seem like you're avoiding the question."

"Maybe I am." She sat up and pulled her knees into her chest, hugging them and still managing to hold her wineglass. "My sisters and I are solid, but my parents? They sort of live in their own worlds. Separate worlds. I guess I might as well tell you because you're bound to hear about it anyway. This reporter, Ariana Lamonte, has been doing a big exposé on my family. My dad mostly. Last year, evidence surfaced that he is actually part of the Fortune family."

Alejandro nodded. "The Fortunes are a big Texas family. Seems like everybody's related to them in one way or another—or at least most people have a close degree of separation. My brother Cisco is married to Delaney Fortune."

Olivia shrugged. "This is still new for me. I'm still trying to digest it, because the implications are pretty damning. Not only does it mean that my father has been lying to us about his identity for as long as my brothers and sisters and I have been alive, but we are also coping with the fact that my father seems to have other children who keep popping up. Illegitimate ones."

She closed her eyes and rested her forehead on her knees. A moment later, she looked up at him.

"I probably shouldn't be telling you all this, but for some crazy reason I feel like I can trust you."

He reached out and put a hand on her arm. "You can trust me, Olivia. It sounds like you've been through a lot of change this year."

She nodded. "Not just this year. The truth has

been a long time coming. I've always known that my parents didn't have a great relationship. I just didn't know why. But now that all of my father's illegitimate children keep crawling out of the woodwork, it's just hard for me to be around my parents. Their relationship is such a farce. I have no idea why they stay together because it's all a lie. So you can see going to dinner with them for my birthday would be the ultimate torture. Will you please be my knight in shining armor and save me from that?"

He brushed back a strand of hair that had fallen into her face. He had heard rumblings about Gerald Robinson's Fortune connection, but nobody seemed to know the true story. He hadn't heard about illegitimate children. No wonder Olivia was freaked out about love and relationships.

"I wouldn't want to do anything else," he said. "You know, love is a tricky thing. My parents showed me the best example of true love and commitment. It was real and perfect. Not only did I see it in my parents' relationship when my mother was alive, I've experienced that deep kind of true love myself. Yet I'm even screwed up when it comes to love. That's because when you fall in love, you're so vulnerable. You open yourself up and you expose yourself to the worst pain—"

The words got lost in his throat. Olivia put her hand on his. He looked at her sitting next to him on the couch in her yoga pants and fitted T-shirt and somehow the possibility of falling in love didn't seem so out of reach anymore.

"Sounds like you're speaking from experience," she said. "How did Anna break your heart?"

It had been years since he'd talked about this, but he heard himself speaking before he could stop himself.

"Anna Molino was my high school sweetheart. We would be married right now if fate hadn't been cruel. Anna died in a car accident when we were just twenty years old."

"Oh, Alejandro, I'm sorry."

Maybe it was all the pent-up emotion that he had been harboring for years; maybe it was because he was actually starting to feel something for this beautiful woman. Whatever the reason, he reached out and ran his thumb along her jawline, moved his hand around so it cupped the back of her neck and lowered his mouth to hers.

When their lips met, he lost all sense of time and space. All he knew was things hadn't felt this right in ages.

"Do you want to stay here tonight?" Olivia whispered. "We can go to the Driskill and get your things tomorrow." Her expression was so earnest, he almost said yes, but if he stayed he wasn't sure what might happen. He needed some space to think about what he was getting into by moving in with her—even if it was only for a week. He needed to figure out if he could handle it.

"In the guest room," she amended as if she was reading his thoughts. "Because we probably shouldn't be kissing like that unless we mean it."

"You're right," he said. "I'm sorry. I shouldn't have done that."

"Don't be sorry," she said. "I'm not. But we probably should save the action for our adoring public."

He stood.

"On that note, I should get back to the hotel tonight."

Chapter Nine

Alejandro checked out of the hotel and was at Olivia's condo by eleven o'clock on Sunday morning. After the kiss last night, she wasn't sure what to expect today. Olivia had even prepared herself for the possibility of Alejandro deciding to stay at the hotel rather than with her.

They were both a little shy this morning as she showed him to the spare bedroom down the hall.

"Here's the closet where you can hang your clothes. I put some extra hangers in there for you. There's a dresser if you need some drawers. I'm sorry this room doesn't have an en suite, but the bathroom is right across the hall. Here, let me show you."

She knew she was talking too much, rambling away like a Realtor showing a house rather than someone welcoming a houseguest. But he wasn't just a houseguest. The thought that she and Alejandro would be sleeping under the same roof made the muscles in her stomach knot a little too tight.

He smiled at her. "This is perfect. Thank you for letting me stay here."

"It's for a good cause. I'll leave you alone while you get settled in. Please let me know if you need anything else to be comfortable. I put fresh towels in the bathroom and—"

"I can unpack later," he said. "What I'd really like to do right now is go get something to eat. Are you hungry?"

She hadn't really thought about it until he'd asked, because she'd been so anxious about whether or not he would end up bailing on her. She put a hand on her stomach and realized that she was famished.

"I am hungry," she said. "Did you have someplace in mind? I would offer to whip us up something but I don't have any food in the house. And that's probably a good thing because I'm not much of a cook."

He laughed. "I was serious last night when I said I was happy to serve as the chef while I'm staying here with you. I might even teach you some of my secrets."

She would love to learn Alejandro Mendoza's secrets, and not just those that pertained to the kitchen. And just like that, all of the potential awkwardness she feared would be spawned from last night's kiss melted away like ice cream on a hot Austin day.

"I'll hold you to that," she said. "Maybe you can give me a cooking lesson tomorrow? But in the meantime why don't we go to the South Congress Café? They have carrot cake French toast that is to die for."

Olivia's condo was just a short walk to the restaurant. It was a beautiful, sunny day, cool enough to make it pleasurable to be outdoors, but warm enough that the walk had Olivia working up a thirst even in the light sundress and sandals she wore.

Alejandro looked crisp and cool in his khaki shorts and ivory linen shirt.

When they arrived at the restaurant they found there was a short wait for a table. This was one of her favorite places to eat and Olivia was happy to see it doing such brisk business.

Even though she'd been there more times than she could count, the place looked both familiar and brand-new as she tried to see the exposed-brick walls and blond-wood-beamed ceilings through Alejandro's eyes.

Once they were seated, Alejandro asked her, "Do you have to do anything constructive today? If not, do you want to order Bloody Marys? One of those would really hit the spot right now."

"I scheduled myself to do absolutely nothing today but recover from the wedding," Olivia said. "A Bloody Mary sounds good, but I think champagne is what I need."

They ordered the drinks along with water and coffee, but asked the server to come back for their food order.

It was nice to be out like this with Alejandro. The pressure of the wedding was off her shoulders, and there was nobody around that they needed to impress. The entire day was theirs. It dawned on Olivia that this was the first time they had been together without any expectations weighing them down.

"I'm guessing that your day is clear since you're drinking?"

He gave a one-shoulder shrug. "For the most part. I have some calls to make later this afternoon. I need to get in touch with my cousin Stefan. He and his brother Rodrigo are my business partners. Since I was basically out of pocket yesterday, I need to go over some things with them."

"Do they live in Miami?" she asked.

"They do."

"Will they be relocating to Austin once you take over Hummingbird Ridge?" That was a clever way of asking whether he'd found a new investor without appearing too nosy.

He shook his head. "Right now, I'm the one who will be in Texas. I know the Dailys so it stands to reason that I would be the one stationed here. Basically Stef and Rod are silent partners. Although I imagine they will want to take a much more hands-on approach once the wine starts flowing."

Well, that sounded encouraging.

"Who wouldn't?" Olivia said. "In fact, if you're ever in need of a taster, I'd be happy to volunteer. It's a tough job, but I am willing to step up and sacrifice myself."

He laughed. "That's magnanimous of you. Not many would sacrifice themselves like that."

Their server reappeared and they ordered—the French toast for Olivia, and the goat cheese and bacon omelet for Alejandro.

"How long have you lived in Austin?" he asked once the server had refilled their water glasses and left to turn in their order.

"All my life. I was born and raised here. I've done a fair share of traveling—you know, study abroad semesters and a postgraduation backpacking trip through Europe. But I keep coming back to Austin. It's home. My life is here. It's where my heart lives. Are you sad to leave Miami?"

"I don't know that I will completely leave. It's hard to say where I'll be after everything is settled with the winery."

Oh.

Disappointment tugged at her insides. She hadn't realized it, but she had been hoping he would say he was eager to call Austin home. It was a crazy thought, though. He was so Miami sophisticated, so big-city, he probably wouldn't be happy here long-term. For all its quirks and artistic originality, Austin had a different vibe from Miami.

"So Miami is home?"

He shrugged. "For now. But less so than it has been. My uncles and cousins still live there, but my father and my immediate family are all in Texas now. As I told you, we're a pretty tight-knit bunch."

"That's nice. Maybe you should think about joining them and making the move. Austin has a lot to offer thanks to the university, and the town has a pretty progressive music scene. Have you ever been to the South by Southwest festival? It's a fabulous film and music festival."

"I know what it is. Or maybe I should say I've heard of it, but I've never been. I'll have to catch it sometime."

"It's always in March. So you just missed it by a couple of months. But there's always next year."

He raised his glass to her. "Here's to next year."

They spent the next ten minutes or so asking personal questions, in a verbal dance of getting to know each other: colleges, careers and craziest things they'd ever done. When their food finally arrived, they ate in the companionable silence that came from good chemistry, each digesting the fresh information they had gleaned—until a familiar voice pulled Olivia out of her reverie.

"Olivia? I thought that was you."

She turned to see Pamela Davis, an accountant at Robinson Tech.

"Hi, Pam. Happy Sunday."

Pamela looked expectantly at Alejandro, obviously waiting for Olivia to introduce her. She was opening her mouth to do just that when the older woman beat her to the punch.

"And this must be your fiancé." Alejandro was a good sport as the woman introduced herself and fawned all over him.

"I was so excited for you when Sophie announced the big news. I had no idea that you were even seeing somebody." Pamela reached out and grabbed Olivia's left hand. "Where's the ring?"

Olivia shot Alejandro a glance. She should have anticipated this. She should simply go to the mall and buy a suitably impressive, but budget-friendly, cubic zirconia because this would surely not be the last time this happened. But then again, if they were going to call off the engagement by this time next week, a ring might complicate matters.

"I wanted to take her to pick out the ring of her dreams," Alejandro said. "We've been so busy with Sophie's wedding that we haven't had a chance to do that yet." He turned to Olivia. "*Querida*, would you like to do that as soon as we finish here?"

"That sounds lovely." For Pamela's benefit, they made googly eyes at each other.

The older woman put her hand over her heart. "Be still, my heart. There's nothing like young love. It makes an old woman like me feel like a kid again. Alejandro, it was so nice to meet you. You take good care of our girl. She's a keeper. And I'm sure you are too if she chose you. I'm going to leave you lovebirds so that you can finish your breakfast and go get that ring. I'll come by your office first thing tomorrow and get a good look at it."

As soon as Pamela cleared the doors of the restaurant, Olivia turned back to Alejandro. "What kind of a fiancé are you to not give me a ring?"

He laughed.

"*Querida*, you heard what I told the lady. We are going right now to pick out the ring of your dreams."

When the dishes were cleared and the server presented the check, Olivia tried to reach for it, but Alejandro was faster. "This is on me."

"Don't be ridiculous," she said. "Please let me split it with you. You need to save your money for that ring."

"Yeah, I'll do that, but this is my treat." He smiled at her. It was a knowing look that made her feel like he could see right through to her soul.

"You can't stand not being in control, can you?" he said.

What was she supposed to say to that? Of course, the answer was yes, but she wouldn't acknowledge it, nor would she admit how she was feeling—as if she and Alejandro had just had their first date.

As they made their way back to her condo, arms bumping and hands brushing occasionally as one or the other slightly leaned into the other's space, they passed a block of storefronts. Olivia paused to linger at the windows. She wasn't in any hurry to get home. Out here they were a man and a woman spending time together, getting to know each other. Once they got back to the condo, he would make his phone calls and she would prepare to return to work tomorrow after being off this week for the wedding. And they would be swept back into their separate lives—separate lives lived under the same roof for the next week. At least she had him to herself right now.

One of the storefronts was an art gallery. They slowed down so she could look at the display cases housing original, handmade jewelry. Earrings and necklaces of hammered silver and burnished metals shared space with ornately rendered rings boasting gemstones of all colors. Olivia caught a glimmer of an exquisite fire opal ring set in an ornately carved rose gold band.

"That's gorgeous," she said, pointing to the ring. "I've always wanted something like that. I'll have to come back and try it on. I'm guessing that you're not a shopper. Am I right?"

"I'm guessing you've got me pegged. But if you want to try it on, you might as well since we're here."

She shook her head. "I don't want to subject you to that torture, because once I start in a shop like that I can't promise how long I'll linger."

She flashed him a flirtatious smile as she started walking away from the shop. "But since we're getting married, maybe that could be my engagement ring."

"Ariana Lamonte of *Weird Life Magazine* is here to see you," Judy Vinson, Olivia's administrative assistant, said over the phone. "I know she doesn't have an appointment, but she asked me to see if you could give her a few moments of your time. She said she's been trying to get in touch with you for more than a month."

"Ugh," Olivia groaned into the phone.

No! Not Ariana Lamonte. The woman was the last person Olivia wanted to see today. It was her first day back and all day she'd felt as if she had been stuck in first gear when she needed to be in fourth to make serious progress toward catching up. Work did not stop even when the boss's daughter got married.

Olivia had already fended off Pamela Davis who, as promised, had appeared in her doorway first thing that morning expecting to see the ring. Olivia was surprised the woman hadn't brought her jeweler's loupe. She stopped her sarcastic thoughts. She was just being defensive because she felt bad for having to tell yet another white lie—this one about the ring being sized.

Lies begat lies. She should be used to that by now. But it didn't mean she had to like it.

Now she had to contend with Ariana Lamonte. The woman was relentless. She had been dogging Olivia for over a month now, trying to pin her down for a meeting. Until now, Olivia had been able to avoid her. Ariana was writing a series of articles about the Fortune family, more specifically about her father's children. She'd been interviewing both the legitimate and illegitimate children of Gerald Fortune Robinson. It was juicy news that Austin's resident genius had sown his seeds far and wide.

"Olivia?" Judy said. "Are you there?"

Olivia sighed loudly. "I'm here, Judy. Look, I can't deal with Ariana Lamonte today. I am drowning in work. Can you get rid of her, please?"

"I'm sorry. Ordinarily, I would have already done that," Judy said, her voice low, "because I know how you feel about her. But I think you might want to talk to her today. She says she has some news that you need to know."

Oh, for God's sake.

Olivia leaned her head back on her chair. If she sent the reporter away, she would only come back. She might as well deal with her once and for all and make the problem go away today.

"Okay, Judy, tell her I'll be with her in a few minutes. I'm going to take a walk with her outside the building. She makes me nervous being in here. Please make sure she stays put. Don't let her wander around. She has a knack for finding the exact place she shouldn't be."

"I hear you," Judy said. "No worries. I have it all under control."

"Thanks, Judy."

Olivia took a moment to smooth her long dark hair—she was wearing it down today. Thank goodness she had taken the extra time to flatiron it smooth. She retouched her powder and reapplied her crimson lipstick. Finally, she stood and smoothed the wrinkles out of her black pencil skirt and white silk buttondown blouse.

If the truth be told, she had put in the extra effort for Alejandro's benefit. Why else would she have subjected her feet to the black stilettos she'd chosen if not to show him her professional side. When she'd walked into the kitchen this morning he'd given her a cup of coffee and a look that said he approved, one hundred percent.

Actually, as painful as the heels could be, they made her feel pulled together and in command. They made her feel badass. So, with that in mind, there couldn't be a better day for Ariana to ambush her.

As Olivia walked down the hall toward the reception area, she chuckled to herself because she really was feeling pretty badass today. That meant the notorious Ms. Lamonte, who thought she could stage this surprise attack, would soon be discovering that the joke was on her.

When Olivia walked into the reception area, she saw a woman who looked to be in her mid to late twenties. She had a curvy figure, long brown hair and dark eyes. Her outfit was boho-artistic. Probably chosen to present an image of creative free spirit meets investigative reporter. She had pretty skin and her makeup accentuated her features but wasn't heavy-handed. She wasn't at all what Olivia had expected. Then again, Olivia didn't know what she had expected when it came to Ariana Lamonte.

But here they were, face-to-face.

Olivia stuck out her hand, immediately taking charge of the situation. "Ms. Lamonte, I am Olivia Fortune Robinson. How can I help you?"

The reporter stood. She was probably close to Olivia's height, but the high-heeled boots she wore made her seem much taller.

"Thanks so much for seeing me. I don't make a habit of showing up unannounced, but I've called several times to set an appointment to no avail. So here I am. I had a feeling this would work."

Ariana tilted her chin up a notch and smiled.

"Yes. I can only give you five minutes because

I'm very busy. I'm in the process of digging myself out after being out of the office all week last week."

Ariana's eyes flashed. "Yes, I know. For your brother's and sister's weddings. I hear the ceremony and reception were absolutely beautiful. And I understand congratulations are in order for you, too. You're engaged! Even though it does seem rather sudden, all of Austin is abuzz with the excitement of the happy news."

It had been less than forty-eight hours since Sophie had opened her big mouth at the wedding and spilled the news. How could "all of Austin" already be abuzz?

"Is that so? You must have some very good inside sources because we haven't announced that news yet. Who told you?"

Ariana widened her eyes and smiled an innocent smile. "Oh, Olivia, surely you know a good reporter never reveals her sources. But I can say this—everyone is very complimentary about your fiancé. I hope I will have the honor of meeting him sometime soon?"

Yeah, not on your life.

"Yes, well, what can I do for you today?"

Ariana hitched her leather handbag up onto her shoulder. "As you know, I have been writing a series called 'Becoming a Fortune.' I was hoping you would allow me to interview you for the next installment."

"Why don't we take a walk, Ariana." Olivia didn't wait for the reporter to weigh in. She simply started walking. "We can talk while we walk."

Olivia cast a glance over her shoulder and saw Ariana stepping double time in those high-heeled boots to catch up. When she did, she fished in her shoulder bag and pulled out a small notebook and pencil.

"What can you tell me about your fiancé?"

Olivia frowned. "He's a very private person, Ariana. I'd rather not talk about him in his absence." They exited the front door of the office building and started walking down the path. "What other questions do you have? If that's it, I really do need to get back to work. I hope you understand."

"Of course. Well, I wanted to ask if you know anything about your father's life before he moved to Austin. I have uncovered some evidence that he may have been married before. Can you tell me anything about that?"

Olivia felt the edges of her peripheral vision go fuzzy for a split second. What? Oh, the fun never ended. Was her mother now going to have to deal with a harem of Gerald Robinson's ex-wives in addition to the flock of illegitimate children? If so, maybe the wives—or *wife*, singular, as Ariana had said—would legitimize some of her father's newfound offspring.

"Ariana, I have no idea what you're talking about. All I know is that my father has been married to my mother for many years. If he had been married to someone else before her I can hardly see how that matters or is any of your business, frankly." She turned on her heels. "I need to get back to work now. For the record, I'd rather not be interviewed. Please don't contact me anymore."

Chapter Ten

Alejandro knew there were many different facets to Olivia, but he'd never seen her quite as overwrought as she was when she got home from work on Monday evening.

"I don't know who Ariana Lamonte thinks she is, but she basically ambushed me at work."

Alejandro poured her a glass of Saint-émilion Grand Cru from the bottle he had opened an hour earlier so that it could breathe for a while.

"Thank you." She took a sip and continued. "Wouldn't you put two and two together and figure out that if somebody didn't return your calls it was a hint that they didn't want to talk to you?"

"I know you mentioned her the other night, but who is this woman?"

"She's a features writer for *Weird Life Magazine*. It's an Austin-based magazine. She's been doing a series of articles called 'Becoming a Fortune.' She is completely obsessed with the Fortunes and all my father's illegitimate offspring."

"Why did she want to interview you?"

"She's been profiling my siblings and basically anyone who has a connection to the Fortunes. I can't believe how many people have cooperated and spoken to her. I don't understand why. It really weirds me out to think that she's putting my father's indiscretions out there for all the world to see."

Olivia sipped her wine. "This is good."

"I thought you might like it. It's one of my favorites. But did you talk to her?"

Alejandro motioned toward the living room. Olivia followed him into the room and they sat on the couch with their wine.

"I tried. Really, I did. But when she started asking about our engagement, that was the beginning of the end. She knows about us, Alejandro, and Sophie spilled the beans less than forty-eight hours ago. She's that obsessed with us."

"How do you think she found out?"

Olivia shrugged, then sipped her wine. "There were a lot of people at the wedding. It could've been anyone really. For all we know, she might be paying someone close to us for information."

"What did you tell her?"

"I shut her down. Changed the subject. And she tried to follow up with the most ridiculous assertion that not only had my dad fathering children with women other than my mother, which we do know is true, but she says she has uncovered evidence that my father was married before he was married to my mother. That was the last straw. I asked her to leave."

"How did she take it?"

"In all fairness, she was actually civil about it. She told me if I didn't want to be interviewed, I didn't have to do it. That's how we left it."

"I'm glad she was decent enough to realize she couldn't force you into something you didn't want to do. Do you think she'll leave you alone?"

"I do. Or at least, I'm hopeful. I think she knows better than to show up at my office again."

"I hope so."

Olivia shook her head and stared off into space for a moment. "Every day it's something new. Some new revelation or surprise about my parents that jumps out and hits me between the eyes. That's why it's easiest to not believe in anything that has to do with love and relationships," she said. "Because just when you think you have a handle on it, that you know what's what, a new piece of evidence surfaces that proves that everything you thought was real and good was all a big lie." She turned to him. "Do you know what it's like to live a charade?"

His right brow shot up. "I'm in the middle of living one right now," he said. "I don't mean to make light of your family situation."

She reached out and touched his hand. "I know you don't. The funny thing is, our relationship feels more real and substantive than anything that my parents have lived for decades."

Her expression softened. And she looked like she had surprised herself by saying it.

"That might've sounded awkward or inappropriate," she said. "I don't mean to put any pressure on you. It's just that you and I are more open and honest with each other than my parents have ever been."

She shook her head and waved her hand as if she were clearing her words from the air.

He wanted to reach out and hold those hands, but he stopped himself. "We are open with each other, Olivia. If I lived in Austin, I think I might want to see if things could work out between us—"

"I was hoping you were still considering moving to Austin. Or at least that Hummingbird Ridge would keep you here for a while, while you look for a new investor."

He silently muttered an explicative. He couldn't tell her that he'd planned to talk to her father about investing, but today he had called Gerald Robinson's assistant and canceled the meeting that was supposed to take place at three o'clock because he didn't want to solicit an investment while he was masquerading as his daughter's fiancé. He didn't want her to feel pressured into intervening or going to bat for him, and he didn't want to seem like one of the many guys who'd used her just to get to her father. But he was going to have to tell her *something* now. "I didn't want to mention this until after the wedding, but that slight snag with the winery purchase is turning out to be more challenging than I first thought."

"What's happened?"

He shook his head, trying to decide how much to tell her. "It's complicated, but it's nothing we can't work out. It's not over yet. I just need some time to reconfigure the timeline. But on a much better note, I have a surprise for you. How about something to brighten your day?"

She narrowed her eyes. "Sounds good to me. What did you have in mind?"

"I got you something. Actually, it's a birthday present, but I'm no good at holding on to gifts. Especially for the better part of a week. It's burning a hole in my pocket. May I give it to you now?"

A smile spread over Olivia's face and some of the stress from the day seemed to melt away. He got up and walked to the kitchen island and came back with a small square red velvet box. Balancing it on his right hand, he offered it to her.

"What is this?" she asked.

"Open it and see."

She held the box for a moment, glancing up at him with a skeptical look on her face. Finally, she opened it.

It was the fire opal ring she had fallen in love with at the shop in downtown Austin yesterday. The sight of it took her breath away.

"Alejandro, what is this?"

He slanted her a glance. "The ring you liked? It is the right one, isn't it?"

"Of course it's the right one." She slid it onto her finger and admired it for a moment before she got up and threw her arms around him. "Why did you do this?"

"It's for your birthday. I guess I should've sung 'Happy Birthday' to you, but I'm sure you would've asked me to stop."

"You shouldn't have done this. It's too much. I know how much it cost."

He shrugged. "Nothing is too good for my fake fiancée. Now when they ask you to see the ring you can show them."

"If I was engaged, this is exactly the ring I would choose."

Olivia framed Alejandro's face with her hands and before she could overthink it, she kissed him.

It was supposed to be a quick thank-you kiss. A peck on the lips to show him her appreciation, but somewhere between *quick* and *kiss*, it turned into something more.

Kissing him had become so natural these days. But this was different. It began leisurely, slowly, starting with a brush of lips and a hint of tongue. But at the contact, reason flew out the window.

When she slid her arms around his neck and opened her mouth, inviting him in, he turned her so that he could deepen the kiss. Deeply, fervently. Desperately.

Olivia fisted her hands in his shirt and pulled him closer.

Her entire body sang. Every sense was heightened as his touch awakened the sensual side of her that had been sleeping for far too long.

She heard the ragged edge of his breathing just beneath the blood rushing in her ears. She felt the heat of his hands on her back. He smelled like heaven: a heady mix of soap and cologne with subtle grassy notes mixed with something leathery and masculine. Yet despite the intoxicating way he smelled, it was the way he tasted—of red wine and something that was uniquely him—that nearly made her drunk with pleasure. The two combined were a heady, seductive mix that teased her senses and made her feel hot and sexy and just a little bit reckless.

Here in his arms, she didn't feel like she had to have control. She wanted to melt into him, let him take charge for a while.

As he tasted and teased, the last bit of reason she possessed took flight. It felt too good to touch him, kiss him. It had been far too long since a man's touch had made her blood churn and her body long to be fully taken.

Was this really about to happen? Was she about to make love to Alejandro? Finally. After pretending to be lovers, they were about to stop lying to themselves. After nights spent dreaming about him, about this, it was about to happen. She wanted it to happen.

Judging by the way he shifted and groaned, he wanted it just as much as she did. His kisses made her body hum, her heart sing. It had been so long since she'd been with anyone and even longer since she had let herself trust anyone the way she trusted Alejandro. She took in a deep breath and squeezed her eyes shut, fighting the wave of feelings swelling inside her, threatening to break.

He untucked her blouse from her pencil skirt and slipped one hand beneath the fabric, the warmth of his hand teasing her bare skin, his fingertips gently caressing her before he grasped the hem of her blouse and pulled it up over her head. She wriggled out of it, helping him by straightening her arms and ducking her head so they wouldn't have to worry about undoing buttons. Next she shed her bra and unzipped her skirt. He pushed her skirt down, taking her panties with it.

Clothing was a barrier and she wanted nothing between them. The realization that they were about to be naked sent a shiver of longing coursing through her.

Sure, they had kissed and touched each other and made everyone around them believe that they were lovers, but this was a new level of intimacy. Skin on skin. This time it was just for them.

But that wasn't going to happen if he remained fully clothed. She tugged his shirt over his head, and let it fall to the floor. Sliding her hands over his bare back, she relished the feel of his muscles beneath her fingertips before going for the button on his pants.

"Alejandro Mendoza, we should've done this a

long time ago," she said, moving her hands down his back and cupping his backside.

"Might've been overkill if it had been a way to prove to Sophie you really do believe in love."

"Seeing is believing."

"I'll say," he conceded.

A half smile curved Olivia's lips. "I had no idea what I was missing." Especially now that she had him completely naked.

He leaned back, his eyes intent on her. "Damn." His voice was hoarse in his throat.

"I'm guessing it's a good thing that I've reduced you to one-syllable words?" she said.

He didn't answer; he simply leaned in and pressed a kiss to the sensitive spot behind her ear, his breath hot and delicious on her neck. Anticipation knotted in her stomach as he walked her backward down the hall toward her bedroom.

Once there, he moved his hand down her hip to her thigh. She parted her legs, and he nestled himself against her.

He kissed her again, moving his hands along the curves of her body. Reaching between her legs, his fingertips traced her sensitive skin, dangerously close to her center, where she was aching for his touch.

Olivia feared she might spontaneously combust or possibly melt into a puddle of her own need right at his feet. And when he finally moved his hand, sliding his finger over her center, she heard a low sound rumbling and realized it was coming from her.

After that, she lost all ability to think lucidly. The

only thing she was aware of was the way Alejandro was teasing the entrance to her body with his fingertip before sliding it deep inside her. Her head lolled back. He increased the rhythm and everything went hot and bright like a sparkler on the Fourth of July. She was electric, sizzling like a live wire or a rocket ship launched into space. And when she finally landed, Alejandro was right there with her, kissing her lips. She could feel the hardness of him pressing against her. He was ready for her.

And she was ready for him. She wanted him so badly she felt she would burst into flames.

He eased her down onto the bed. Everything that was dark about his eyes grew even darker.

"Do you have a condom?" he said.

"Me? No, I don't have any." There had been no need. Until now. Oh, for God's sake, why hadn't they thought about this before now? Why? Because they had sworn this wasn't going to happen. A hiccup of laughter nearly escaped her lips. Just making that promise should have been her first clue that she needed to have some on hand. She supposed she should've been relieved that he hadn't come prepared because that would've meant he'd been planning this seduction. But, good grief, if they had come this far and had to stop for lack of protection, she just might actually die.

"I may have one in my shaving kit. If I do, I don't know how old it is, though."

"Not much action lately, huh?"

He groaned and kissed her. "I'm not quite sure

how you want me to answer that. Still, it's worth a look. I'll be right back."

She watched him walk across the room naked and fine. Funny, she thought, you can tell yourself you're immune, you can tell yourself you don't want something or you shouldn't have something, when all the while the *don'ts* and *shouldn'ts* are a colossal lie. Seeing him like this, she knew she had been lying to herself since the night she saw him in the Driskill Hotel bar.

She wanted him. And on some very basic level, she'd known they were going to end up like this— whether she'd wanted to admit it to herself or not.

Olivia turned over onto her side and drew in a deep, measured breath, trying to calm her shallow breathing and slow her thudding heart.

This is happening. This is really happening.

And she couldn't believe how right it felt. It was probably going to make things harder when he went back to Miami; she was well aware of that. But she had known it would be difficult from that first moment, after that first kiss, when they'd started down this thrilling, rocky road. But the thing was, even after that first kiss, things had never been awkward. Even the public displays of intimacy they'd put on for Sophie's benefit hadn't been awkward. In fact, the lack of awkwardness had blurred the line between fantasy and reality that should've been so distinct. She could only hope this wasn't a mistake, that after all was said and done, making love to Alejandro wouldn't be the straw that brought everything crashing down.

He returned a moment later, holding a small square packet.

"Victory is ours," he said. "And it is still well within its shelf life. I am happy we can give it a decent burial."

Olivia propped herself up on her elbow and laughed at the double meaning. "I never dreamed a rubber could make me so happy."

"You obviously need to expand your horizons, *querida*."

She loved how he called her that. The endearment warmed her from the inside out. As if she could be any hotter right now.

"What I meant was, it would've been a real mood killer if you would've had to have gotten dressed and gone to the drugstore."

He ripped open the foil packet.

"No worries. This time. We might want to keep that in mind for the future, though."

The future.

The thought caused Olivia's heartbeat to kick up again. Would there be a next time? She hoped so. But why was she thinking about next time before *this time* had even happened. And it was about to happen.

It had been a long time since she'd been intimate with a man, but he was worth the wait.

She watched, mesmerized, as Alejandro positioned the condom over himself and rolled it down his hard length. Arousal ripped through her, knocking the breath right out of her lungs. But that was nothing compared to when Alejandro slid into bed next to her and, with one swift motion, had her lying flat on her back.

Alejandro kissed her senseless. It was as if his next breath depended on it. Need had her fisting her fingers in the hair at the nape of his neck until he grabbed ahold of her wrists and lifted her arms over her head. He deepened the kiss and positioned himself between her thighs, his hard manhood bumping against the private entrance to her body. And suddenly she needed him inside her.

His gaze locked on hers, he thrust gently to fill her. She raised her hips to take him all the way in. His breath escaped in a rush, and he held absolutely still for a moment, as if he were afraid to break the fragile moment of their joining. Looking into his eyes, Olivia reveled in the sensation, in the wonder of this man inside her.

"You feel even better than I imagined," he whispered, his voice sounding hoarse and raspy.

His eyes were the darkest shade of brown she'd ever seen. As he moved inside her, she couldn't take her eyes off him. He pulled back slightly just before thrusting deeper, closing those dark eyes, getting lost in the rhythm of their love.

The driving need that led to her release grew with every pump and thrust. She held on to him, watching him, his expression, his eyes squeezed shut, his jaw clenched tight.

This was Alejandro. Gorgeous, sexy Alejandro. And he was lost in her.

She looked away, unable to deal with the intensity as he pushed into her one last time and she caught a glimpse of his tattoo. That tattoo. Another woman's name branded on his arm. She turned her face away so she wouldn't have to see it, wouldn't have to think about him in love with someone else.

She refocused on the passion, on how right they felt together, on the feel of him moving inside her, and the next moment pleasure exploded within her, and she felt as if the clouds had parted on a gray day and she was looking directly into the sun.

His eyes closed and his neck tendons strained as the orgasm shook his body. She slid her hands along the rock-hard muscles of his arms to end up with her fingers curled into his hair. He swayed above her for a moment before she pulled him down on top of her. He bowed his head and rested his forehead on hers, kissing her again as if drawing a sustaining life's breath from the final moments of their coupling.

He rolled off her onto his back and she curled herself into his body, amazed by the heat radiating from his skin.

He covered his eyes with his palms. Then, keeping his elbows crooked, he slid his hands beneath his head. She wasn't sure if this was the right thing to do. Her instincts were telling her to hold on to him, snuggle into him, because that's what lovers did after making love. But he wasn't making any effort to hold her. As right and intuitive as the lovemaking had been, this part felt awkward.

The last thing she wanted was for her vulnerability to morph into neediness. Because that was so not who she was. She had never been a clinging vine. And she didn't want to start now.

But, dammit, she felt clingy.

She didn't want to have feelings for him. He made her want things that didn't make sense. Things that she didn't even believe in. He was part of the extended family. She had even hoped after their short-term engagement that they could be friends.

Family and friendship. Those things were far too valuable to mess up. Why was she just considering that now?

She supposed that somewhere deep in her psyche she thought making love to him would exorcise whatever demon had possessed her when she met him. While it had been mind-blowing, it hadn't satisfied that craving. No, she still wanted more. She needed more. She wondered if rather than satisfying the beast, she had simply awakened it.

She lay there lost in thought, heart thundering as she tried to sort out her emotions.

"You okay?" he asked.

She nodded, but he didn't say more. They just lay next to each other, until she couldn't stand the silence anymore. She turned over onto her side, facing him. She stared at him through the golden early-evening light, filtering in through the bedroom's plantation shutters.

Olivia studied his profile as he lay there with his arm raised over his head, his tattoo in full view. She reached out and touched it. She hadn't pushed him to talk about it the other night because it'd felt too personal, as if she were crossing the line. But here they were in the most emotionally vulnerable space. It felt like nothing should be off-limits.

"Tell me about Anna."

He was silent for a long time, and for a moment she thought he wasn't going to answer her.

But she wanted to know. She needed to know. So she decided to prod him.

"You loved her." The words escaped before she could stop herself and she felt awkward after saying them, because obviously he had loved Anna and he didn't love her.

"I did. I still do. I have to be honest with you, I always will."

Olivia felt small, and irrationally jealous of the dead woman.

"We met in our freshman year of high school in English class. Anna was new to the school. She'd just moved to Miami from Venezuela. We were reading *Romeo and Juliet* aloud in class. She read Juliette's part and I read Romeo's. It was love at first sight. I was so taken by her grace and beauty, I wanted to marry her when we turned eighteen. I'd even saved my money and bought her an engagement ring. But Anna's father asked us to wait to get married until after we'd graduated from college. We weren't happy about it, but we honored his wishes. It was important

to Anna. But we still got engaged. We ended up going
to different universities—she was at Florida State in
Tallahassee and I was at the University of Florida in
Gainesville. We alternated weekend visits, taking
turns making the drive to see each other. Sophomore
year, she was killed instantly when a semitruck driver
fell asleep at the wheel and hit her car.

"I have always felt responsible for her death. If
only I had insisted she leave Sunday afternoon when
it was still light outside rather than staying one more
night with me and leaving before sunrise the next
morning to make it back for an early class."

She heard the pain in his voice, but it was her pain
she felt when he said the next words.

"I guess I've always believed each person was only
granted one true love in a lifetime. I always believed
Anna was mine."

He lowered his arm, held it in front of him, trac-
ing the intricate lines etched into his skin.

"I got her name tattooed on my arm so that I would
always remember that once life wasn't hard and happiness wasn't impossible."

She wanted to ask, *What do you think now? Do
you think you could be happy with me?* But she
couldn't force the words out of her throat.

Chapter Eleven

The following Saturday was Olivia's birthday. Alejandro had planned a perfect birthday celebration for her—a feast featuring filet mignon and butter-poached lobster, and of course it would be accompanied by continuously flowing champagne since it seemed to be Olivia's favorite. And flowers. Lots of flowers. The condo looked like he had robbed a florist. Even though he had given Olivia her birthday present, the fire opal ring, earlier that week, he'd sent her out to the spa to be pampered so that she could relax and he could prepare for their romantic evening in.

During the day, while she was at work, Alejandro had been spending time at Hummingbird Ridge, proceeding as if the deal was still on track despite the

fact that they'd suspended the closing indefinitely—
or at least until he could secure another source of
funding. It was difficult knowing he had a poten-
tially untapped investor in Gerald. But he had to bide
his time.

He could not give the impression that he had proposed to Olivia to get the inside track on securing
the deal. His conscience simply wouldn't let him do
that. He had to wait until after Olivia broke up with
him. If she was the one to walk away, Gerald would
know that he hadn't broken Olivia's heart, and Olivia
would know that he hadn't been like every other guy
who had seen an opportunity and used her to further
his ambitions. His new plan was to talk to Gerald first
and see whether he was interested. If Gerald decided
to invest in Hummingbird Ridge, Alejandro would
talk to Olivia and explain why he had done things the
way he had done them. She would be off the hook and
wouldn't feel beholden to him for helping her with
the Sophie debacle.

Technically they wouldn't be together, wouldn't be
dating or engaged or be lovers— Okay, so they were
lovers. That was the one part of the equation that was
real. Maybe he should've exercised some restraint and
waited until all the pretense was over, all the business
deals were closed, and then they could've entered into
a relationship of their own volition, but it was pretty
clear he had no restraint when it came to Olivia.

Once everything was settled and Hummingbird
Ridge was his, Alejandro would move to Austin and
he had every intention of starting over and dating

Olivia the right way, treating her the way she deserved to be treated.

He had just taken a pound of butter out of the refrigerator to make a compound butter for the fresh French bread he had purchased when he heard someone entering the condo.

"Hello?" he said.

"Hey, it's me." Olivia was home about an hour earlier than he was expecting her and judging by her expression something wasn't right.

"What's wrong?" He walked over and kissed her.

"I hope dinner can keep."

"Why?"

"Sophie and Mason decided to come back from their honeymoon a day early because of bad weather," she said. "There's this tradition in our family, that we have a big dinner to welcome the newlyweds home their first night back from their honeymoon. That means we are cordially invited to my parents' at six o'clock this evening. Attendance will be taken."

Alejandro raked his hand through his hair. "How can they expect us? Can't you tell them we already have plans? It's your birthday."

"Coming home from your honeymoon trumps a birthday, I'm afraid," she replied. "Besides, when my mother called, she said we would be celebrating my birthday tonight along with Sophie and Mason's return. So she gets her way after all. Should've known. She always does."

Alejandro frowned. "But how can they pull together a dinner party on such short notice?"

"The plans have been in place since before the wedding. The menu was planned, the flowers, the decorations, the tablescapes, the guest list. Even though it was planned for tomorrow night. Oh, I guess I forgot to tell you about that, didn't I? Sorry. If it makes you feel any better, there will be another dinner when Dana and Mason get back next week. Just be glad you won't have to attend that one."

What she didn't say was: *You won't have to attend because by that point we will be broken up.*

The unspoken words hung between them.

He thought he saw regret and sadness in her eyes, but maybe he was just projecting his own feelings onto her. The plan was to break up after Sophie and Mason returned. He needed that to happen so he could execute the next phase of his plan. However, Olivia told him about the dinner tradition. Probably because she had no idea that he was trying to avoid her father. The two of them had bonded over a joke of avoiding her parents for a completely different reason than the one that had him steering clear of Gerald. It appeared that he would have no choice but to go tonight. Unless—

"We haven't really talked about the logistics of our breakup," he said. "Maybe it would facilitate matters if I didn't go tonight."

He knew it was a bad idea before Olivia started shaking her head. That's when he realized how weary she looked.

"I know it's a lot to ask, and I've already asked way too much of you." She looked too vulnerable and tired. "Can you just hang in there one more night? If I go without you, the attention will be focused on where you are and why we aren't together. Not only will it detract from Sophie and Mason's homecoming, but..."

She stared at her hands for a moment. When she looked up at him again, that's when he noticed that she had tears glistening in her eyes.

"It's my birthday, Alejandro. It's bad enough that I won't get to celebrate the way I want to, but I really don't want to break up on my birthday."

They were supposed to start the evening in the living room with drinks and hors d'oeuvres and a toast to the newlyweds and Olivia.

She had asked her mother if they could just focus on Sophie and Mason tonight. After all, her birthday happened once a year; her little sister only returned from her honeymoon once in her lifetime. But when Charlotte Robinson had a plan, no one changed her mind. That stubborn streak was probably what had kept her married to Gerald all these years. She lived in one of the largest homes in Austin; she had money and a lofty position in Texas high society. Those things mattered to Charlotte. Olivia supposed that was why she stayed with her husband despite the humiliation of everyone knowing that he had not only cheated on her repeatedly, but had flesh and blood souvenirs from those dalliances. Souvenirs who shared his DNA.

Compared to that, a birthday party was inconsequential. Still, Charlotte wasn't about to change the plans and forget tonight was Olivia's birthday. It didn't matter what Olivia wanted as long as Charlotte could put on airs and pretend like everything was fine.

Olivia led Alejandro down the polished wooden hallway to the first door on the left—the living room—and they joined a handful of family members who were already there. Sophie and Mason had arrived and were sipping champagne and happily mingling with the others.

Olivia wished she and Alejandro could stay in the background, that they could be flies on the wall and observe the festivities from a safe distance, because talk was bound to meander to the engagement. Olivia's thumb found the back of the fire opal ring Alejandro had given her for her birthday. The makeshift engagement ring burned her finger. As much as she loved it she wanted to take it off and stuff it in her purse. She loved that ring, but with everyone oohing and ahhing over the gorgeous stone, she wondered if she would be able to look at it the same way after Alejandro returned to Miami and she resumed her life. Funny, she used to feel she had a full life, a fulfilling life—no one to answer to, no one to consider, no one to make her realize she really did lead a small and lonely existence that consisted of getting up in the morning alone, working sixteen-hour days, coming home and falling into bed alone, only to get up in the morning and do it all over again. She was twenty-eight years old and this was all she had to show for herself. She balled her hand into a fist so she couldn't see the ring.

A server stopped in front of her and Alejandro with a tray of champagne. He grabbed two flutes and handed her one. The two of them locked gazes before they toasted each other. She wondered if he was thinking the same thing that she was thinking—that yes, the sex had been great. Mind-blowing, in fact.

In that instant, he slipped his arm around her, falling so naturally into the part he had been playing so well, and she knew she didn't want it to end. She didn't want to tell everyone the engagement was off, that they had broken up. She encircled his waist with a possessive arm. Because somewhere along the line Alejandro Mendoza had proven to her that there were decent men left in the world. Men who were trustworthy. Men who didn't use you for your father's wealth and your family's social standing. In fact, this man had selflessly helped her and wanted absolutely nothing in return.

And now he was about to walk out of her life.

They were too good together for her to let him go without knowing exactly what he meant to her, what she felt for him. She had to have faith that he was starting to feel the same way. Because how in the world could two people be so good together and not want to last?

It would be her birthday present to herself. Tonight, after they got home, she would tell him exactly how she felt.

She smiled at him and he leaned down and kissed

her. It was just a quick, whisper-soft kiss, but it filled her heart and nourished her entire being.

"Olivia!" Sophie said, coming up to them and huddling in close so that no one else could hear. "Look at you two. If this is still an act for my benefit, I do beg you to stop. I mean, I appreciate all the trouble you went to, but look at you two." She turned to Mason. "Honey, besides us, have you ever seen two people who are more perfect for each other?" She turned back and whispered to Alejandro, "Please tell me the two of you have figured that out."

Sophie and her exuberance. You had to hand it to her. Only, Olivia wished that all this enthusiasm was coming after she'd had a chance to talk to Alejandro, because she wasn't quite sure what to say. Of course, the plan was to keep up the ruse through tonight. Alejandro had been so gracious about not spoiling her birthday by staging the breakup tonight. So all she had to do was tell Sophie of course they were in love, just like they always had been, and always would be.

Until the breakup.

All she had to do was open her mouth and say it—except for the part about the breakup. That would come soon enough. Unless it didn't. But pretending tonight made Olivia fear that it might jinx everything.

They were here, together. The less said the better.

Before she could say anything, Sophie took Olivia's left hand and lifted it up. She gasped at the fire opal. "This is new. This is beautiful. Is this the engagement ring? Because if it is, I am starting to believe that this game you've been playing might in fact be real. Please tell me it's real and you two really are in love."

Before she could answer, her parents joined them. They were making the rounds greeting their guests, pretending to be the perfect host and hostess. Olivia wanted to roll her eyes and say to her sister, *If you want an act, talk to the two of them. They are insufferable.*

"Hello, Alejandro, I'm Charlotte, Olivia's mother. I'm sorry we haven't had the opportunity to formally meet before now." Charlotte extended her hand as if she expected Alejandro to kiss it. He did, and somehow he made it look so incredibly natural and genuine.

"It's nice to meet you, Mrs. Robinson. Thank you for allowing me to join in the celebration tonight."

"You're family, Alejandro. Of course you would be included this evening. I'm sure very soon we will be planning a similar party for you and Olivia."

Gerald had been talking to Mason while Charlotte had been addressing Alejandro. As if perfectly choreographed, they switched. Olivia's stomach knotted as Gerald zeroed in on Alejandro.

But she was confused when her father said, "He does exist. I was beginning to think that you were a figment of my imagination since Olivia doesn't make a habit of bringing many men home. Or, after you canceled our meeting, I thought maybe the Hummingbird Ridge deal had completely fallen through and you had left town."

"Meeting?" Olivia said. "What were you two meeting about?"

"Alejandro here has a business proposal for me. I did some investigating and I learned that a large portion of his financing for Hummingbird Ridge fell through. I'm guessing he wants me to plug the gap. I was interested." He turned to Alejandro. "But I must admit I'm a little skeptical since you haven't shown very good follow-through."

Olivia's blood ran cold. She looked at Alejandro. "Are you going to ask my father to invest in your business?"

Alejandro looked panicked, but when he nodded the edges of Olivia's vision turned red.

"I'm getting ready to leave on a business trip day after tomorrow," Gerald said to him. "If you're serious about this you need to get in before I go. Otherwise I think the window of opportunity is closed. The only reason I'm giving you a second chance is because of Olivia. If she loves you, that has to speak to your character. And if you marry her you'll need to be able to support her in the manner in which she is accustomed."

So Alejandro Mendoza was no better than any of the others. Oh, wait, yes he was. He was much smoother. He had actually convinced her that she could trust him.

"Excuse me," she said, fighting back hot, angry tears. "I need to leave. I'm not feeling well."

Alejandro excused himself and went after Olivia. Sophie came after her, too, but Alejandro said, "If you don't mind, I'd like to talk to her privately."

"Is she okay?" Sophie asked. "I don't understand what just happened."

Alejandro didn't try to explain. "Liv, please wait, please," he said, and went after her. Sophie must've stayed back, because he was alone as he stepped out the front door and made his way to the driveway where he caught up with her. "Will you please let me explain? Because I can explain."

"I'm sure you can," she said. "The only problem is I don't want to hear it. However, I do need you to take me home. Or if you'd rather, I can call for an Uber. But you will need to come and get your things tonight so you might as well drive me. Unless you'd like to go in and see how much money you can get out of my father."

That hurt. But he knew from her point of view she thought he deserved it.

"Get in the car and I'll explain."

Miraculously, she complied. Once they were inside he said, "It's true, I did ask your father for a meeting to discuss investing in Hummingbird Ridge. But I asked him before you and I got serious. That day at the winery when we were there for the tasting, I got a call from my cousin telling me that one of the key investors had pulled out of the deal. Minutes earlier, I'd been talking to Gerald and he had been saying that he was intrigued by the Texas wine industry and had been looking into investing. After I got the call—actually, before we left Hummingbird Ridge—I asked him if I could meet with him to discuss possible investment opportunities. I scheduled an appointment for Monday. This past Monday. At three o'clock. But after things took a turn and everyone thought we were engaged, I canceled the meeting with him. I canceled because I didn't want to go into that meeting under false pretenses."

"But you're still going to meet with him. You made love to me knowing full well you have a plan. Otherwise you would've told me about it. Why didn't you tell me, Alejandro?"

She sat there with her arms crossed, walls up, glaring at him, a mixture of hurt and rage contorting her tearstained face.

"I didn't tell you because I didn't want you to feel like you had to intervene, or feel like I was using you. Because I wasn't, Olivia. I didn't want you to know anything about it until it was a done deal. I didn't want you to think my business deal with your father had any bearing on us or that I expected anything from you."

She shook her head. "But don't you see it has everything to do with us? You kept it a secret. You went behind my back and didn't tell me—"

Her voice broke. He reached out to touch her and she shook him off.

"Liv, please."

"Alejandro, we were going to break up after Sophie and Mason got back anyway. This is as good a time as any to end it. Please take me home and we can both get on with our lives."

Chapter Twelve

"Olivia, open up. I know you're in there."

Sophie's voice sounded between the bouts of intermittent knocking.

"Olivia, if you don't open the door I'm going to call the police to do a safety check," she continued. No, wait, that sounded like Rachel.

"Don't test us, because we mean it." And there was Zoe.

All three of her sisters were standing outside her condo door. Experience reminded her that they were absolutely serious about calling the police. They would do it. This wasn't a mere battle of wills. It was three Fortune Robinson sisters against one. There was no winning that battle.

Olivia dragged her yoga pant-clad self off the

couch, raked a hand through her tangled hair and opened the door.

"Why aren't you three at work?"

They glanced at each other. "Because it's Sunday?" Zoe offered.

Was it only Sunday? Yikes. Time really did stand still when you had a broken heart. Since Alejandro had left, she had been dozing on and off, in and out of a fitful, tearful, nightmare-laden sleep. She'd confined herself to the couch, because she couldn't make herself sleep in the bed that she and Alejandro had shared the previous week, the bed in which they had made love. The bed in which she had given herself to him body and soul.

She was such an idiot.

How had she allowed herself to fall for him? To be so taken in, so gullible, so ready to believe that he was different from any of the other jerks who had used her.

She looked at her sisters, all three of them happily married to good, decent men. Sure, they'd had their own challenges when it came to finding true love, but never like she'd had.

What was wrong with her?

A saying came to mind. *If every guy in the whole world uses you, maybe it's not every guy in the whole world who has a problem.*

It went something like that, some permutation of that. But it didn't matter if she'd mentally quoted it exactly. She got the gist.

Apparently not every guy in the whole world was

a scumbag since her sisters were all happily married. So that meant something was wrong with her that she kept attracting the users.

Zoe held up the doughnut box and smiled. "We brought you something. They're birthday doughnuts, since you didn't get cake yesterday."

"I'll make coffee," Rachel offered.

"I'll help Olivia wash her face," Sophie said.

Like a child, Olivia allowed her sister to shepherd her into the bathroom. Olivia caught a glimpse of herself in the mirror and winced. She looked like hell. She hadn't bothered to take off her makeup after Alejandro left. Her tears had washed away most of it, but there were still vague brown and black streaks where her mascara had meandered down her cheeks, mixing with her foundation and bronzer.

Sophie opened the bathroom linen closet and took out a washcloth. She wet it and gently blotted Olivia's face.

"Rough night?" she asked.

Olivia shrugged, not quite sure what to say. Because really what could she say? Sophie would probably think this was what she deserved. Maybe her sisters were right. Maybe her bad attitude was what drew the negative to her. Maybe because she expected all men to be the same, the ones she met were exactly that.

But she had let herself believe that Alejandro was different.

Dear God, what a mistake that had turned out to be.

"Where's your ring?" Sophie asked.

Olivia tamped down the irritation that sprang to life at Sophie's question.

Have you not been paying attention? The words strained and pawed at the tip of her tongue, but somehow, in the haze of her grief, she knew better than to unleash them.

"I gave it back to Alejandro. I don't need it anymore."

Actually, what she had done was return it to the little red box it'd come in and slide it into his briefcase when he had been in the guest room packing. She knew he would've never accepted it if she had handed it to him. But she couldn't keep it when all it would do was serve as a reminder of how he had broken her heart.

"You know, in Texas some courts have said that the woman is allowed to keep the ring if the guy breaks off the engagement."

Olivia frowned and blinked up at Sophie. "And why do you know this?"

"Who knows? I heard it somewhere and my brain has a knack for hanging on to useless information. I probably retained it for the same reason I can still sing every single word of *Sesame Street*'s 'Rubber Duckie' song. Want me to sing it for you? Would that make you happy?"

Olivia held up her hand. "That's okay. Really."

But the joke made Olivia smile. Her sisters. What would she do without them? Especially sweet Sophie, who should be spending this Sunday with her new husband, not helping her spinster sister nurse her broken heart. The warmth she felt at the gesture began to sting her eyes and soon the tears had started again.

God, she hated feeling out of control like this.

Sophie grabbed her into a hug. "Oh, Liv, I'm so sorry you're hurting. You really do love him, don't you?"

Adding to the out-of-control feeling, she realized she was nodding her head when she should've been shaking it and convincing herself that she didn't love him.

"I know your relationship started off as a ruse to get me back in the wedding, but from the minute I saw the two of you together I was holding out for you. I knew this was real even if you all didn't know it."

She wanted to tell Sophie to stop. It was over. She'd loved and lost and now her heart was broken and she didn't want to talk about it anymore. Rehashing everything was only making it worse. Salt in the wound. Insult to injury.

"Olivia, if you love him, why are you sitting here? Why are you letting him get away? I don't even understand what happened last night."

The two of them sat down on the edge of the jetted tub. Olivia found her voice and gave Sophie the lowdown.

Sophie listened without saying a word until Olivia had talked herself out. When she was quiet, Sophie said, "Okay, let me get this straight. You're upset with him about a winery deal that he already had going before he met you. The one that would keep him here in Austin. And you're upset because he intended to ask our father to buy in to save the deal, but he put off asking him because he didn't want to approach dad under false pretenses and he didn't want to involve you because he didn't want you to feel obligated to help him after you had roped him into this wedding farce he gained absolutely nothing from. Hmm... Let's think about that for a minute."

Sophie let the words hang in the air.

"I don't know, Liv. I'm not quite seeing the same picture of a liar and a scoundrel and a cheat that you seem to think he is. Am I missing something?"

"Yeah, I'm not seeing it, either," Rachel said. Olivia looked up to see Rachel and Zoe standing in the bathroom doorway. "I think you're in love and you're scared. I think you're projecting your fears onto him so that the relationship will end and you'll be exactly where you thought you would be."

Olivia sucked in a quick breath.

"Well, congratulations," said Zoe. "You did it. You wanted him to leave. And he did. Happy now?"

"Zoe, *shush*," said Rachel.

"No, she's right," said Olivia. "She's absolutely one-hundred-percent right. I've been so busy wallowing in my misery over being left, over thinking any man who is interested in me is a scoundrel who wants something. But that's not Alejandro. I may have lost the best thing that's ever happened to me, because I'm an idiot."

"No, you're not an idiot," said Sophie. "You are a smart, wonderful, generous person with a huge heart.

You will go to the ends of the earth for those you love. You proved that in what you did for me. Now be kind to yourself and go after him. Go get your man."

"I will," Olivia said. "I mean, I would, but I don't know where he is."

"He didn't tell you where he was going?" Rachel asked.

"He had to sleep somewhere last night. Obviously he didn't go to his brothers, because you would know if he had. He didn't stay with Cisco and Delaney. Maybe he went back to the Driskill?"

"Let me get my cell phone and I'll look up the number and we can call and see if he's registered there," said Zoe. "Rachel, you call Cisco and ask if he's there."

"Or we could just call his cell phone," Sophie said.

Of course. Why hadn't she thought of that? It was the only logical thing to do, but her brain had been so addled she hadn't even considered the obvious.

Olivia got her phone and called Alejandro's number. When it started ringing, they heard a strange ringing sound coming from the spare bedroom. The four of them went to investigate and finally found Alejandro's cell phone underneath the foot of the bed. It must've fallen out of his pocket as he was packing.

Olivia sighed. "Well, now I have a valid reason to see him again."

"Olivia, your feelings for him are a valid reason to see him again," said Zoe. "You need to think positively. As positively about the outcome of things for yourself as you do for those you love. Because you are worth it. You deserve the same kind of love that you bestow upon other people."

After her sisters left, Olivia sat in the silent living room for a long time thinking. Rachel had called her husband, Matteo, and had gotten the phone numbers of Rodrigo and Stefan, Alejandro's cousins and business partners.

Now Olivia placed a call to Stefan.

"Hi, Stefan, this is Olivia Fortune Robinson. I'm a friend of Alejandro's. He was staying with me in Austin while he was here for the wedding."

"Hey, Olivia, I know who you are. Alejandro had a lot of nice things to say about you."

Her heart clenched. He had nice things to say about her, but she'd thought the worst of him. Well, he probably wasn't thinking nice things about her now. With just cause.

"He left Austin yesterday and I'm not sure where he went, but he left his cell phone here and I'd like to get in touch with him to let him know I have it. Is he back in Miami, by any chance?"

"No, he's still in Texas. He went to see his dad in Horseback Hollow. If you want, you can probably get in touch with him through Orlando."

Stefan gave Olivia the telephone number.

"Stefan, can you tell me a little bit about Hummingbird Ridge? As an investment...and what you're looking for in an investor. I know that one of your investors pulled out. Can you give me a ballpark dollar amount? I may know someone who is looking for an investment opportunity."

It was a whim, and she knew a whim could be dangerous because, as a general rule, spontaneity had always gotten her in trouble. But then again so had planning everything out to the last painstaking detail. So she took a deep breath and threw caution to the wind.

He filled her in on the details.

"Thanks so much, Stefan. I'll get back with you. Or Alejandro when I see him."

"Hey, no problem. It's nice to talk to the woman who has stolen my cousin's heart."

Alejandro had confided his feelings in Stefan?

The thought renewed her hope.

She called Alejandro's phone. She knew he wouldn't pick up, but that was beside the point. She wanted to hear his voice. That's all she meant to do— call, listen to his voice on his voice mail greeting and hang up. Instead, she ended up leaving him a message, even though she knew he wouldn't get it until she gave him back his phone.

"Alejandro, it's Olivia. I'm sorry. What I hate most about this fight is that I might've ruined something that could've been so good. I hope that we can talk about this. Will you give me that chance? Because if I don't get the chance to tell you I love you, I know I'll regret it for the rest of my life. I love you."

He might not want to hear from her. He might want her to mail the phone to him since he would probably be back in Miami soon. But she had to tell him how she felt.

Since Rachel lived in Horseback Hollow, and Stefan said Alejandro was there… If he was still going to be there tomorrow when her sister went home, maybe Rachel could take the phone to him. Or maybe Olivia could go with her and deliver it herself.

One way or another he had to hear her message.

Alejandro should've trusted his instincts. If he hadn't gone to the party, Gerald wouldn't have had the opportunity to dump on them like that in front of Olivia. But who was he kidding? If he hadn't gone to the party, Olivia would've gone by herself and her father probably would've sent a message home through her about what a flake he was for canceling the meetings and avoiding him.

In hindsight, he should have been upfront with Olivia. He could've told her he didn't want her to get involved in his offer to her father. If only he could go back and do it over again. But he couldn't. He had to deal with the way things were. He needed to focus on finding another investor for Hummingbird Ridge.

On his way out of Austin to Horseback Hollow he had stopped by the winery. Jack and Margaret Daily had agreed to give Alejandro first right of refusal if another buyer came along. That motivated him to quit moping and get the job done.

In the meantime, it was good to be sitting at the Hollows Cantina in Horseback Hollow having a beer with his father before returning to Miami.

"I'm sorry the engagement is off," Orlando said.

Alejandro waited for his father to add that everything had happened too fast and they'd probably gotten caught up in the moment, but he didn't. They sat in companionable silence not needing to talk, just happy to be in each other's company.

Alejandro had already decided that he wouldn't tell his father that everything started off as a farce, a ruse to get Sophie down the aisle, and somehow it had turned into something real. That, for the first time since Anna, he had been able to feel again.

"You love her," Orlando said as if reading his mind.

"Yep."

"Then what are you doing here when you should be there telling her that?"

By the time Olivia talked to Orlando, Alejandro had already left Horseback Hollow.

Her heart sank. Orlando hadn't been very forthcoming with information about Alejandro's whereabouts. She couldn't blame him; after all, he was protecting his son. However, he had promised to relay the message to Alejandro that she had called and she had his phone.

It should've been enough, leaving messages with both Stefan and Orlando, but Olivia spent a restless Sunday night tossing and turning and coming up with a crazy plan. By six o'clock Monday morning she was at Austin–Bergstrom International Airport, boarding a flight to Miami.

Rachel was the only person she told of her plan. Olivia knew it was a crazy thing to do, but she had never been the type to sit around and wait for things to happen. In fact, when it came to love she had pro-actively prevented anything from happening. Not this time. When she went to bed tonight, she would know that she had done everything possible to save the best thing that had ever happened to her.

When she landed in Miami armed with Alejandro's address, she got a cab to his house. The only problem was Alejandro wasn't there. He wasn't at his office, either. That's where she met Stefan and Rodrigo in person. They told her he was still in Texas.

"But Orlando said he left," she told them.

His cousins seemed truly baffled. Or maybe they were just good actors covering for him—after all, his acting ability might run in the family. Maybe he didn't want to see her and his family was running interference.

She tried to leave his cell phone with them, but they refused. "I know he has a meeting at Hummingbird Ridge at the end of the week," Stefan said. "I think you would be better off taking the phone back with you. He can pick it up from you when he's there. If he needs a cell in the meantime, he can get one of those disposable phones."

"If he does, would you please let me know the number?"

She sounded desperate, even to her own ears. Well, she was desperate.

Maybe Alejandro was right. Maybe true love only came around once in a lifetime. He'd had his with Anna. Olivia had found hers—as short-lived as it had been—with him.

Olivia and her bruised heart returned to Miami International Airport. Disappointment was her only companion. Instead of leaving with the fulfillment—or at least the closure—she was certain she'd find when she saw Alejandro and he realized the great lengths that she would go to for him, she left feeling uncertain and small.

By the time she landed in Austin, it was nearly seven thirty in the evening. She was tired and she should be hungry, but she wasn't. All she wanted to do was go home and put on her jammies and pull the covers over her head.

She was intently digging in her purse for her car keys as she exited the airport and she wasn't really watching what she was doing.

"Excuse me, miss. Do you need a ride?"

In the split second before she could fully register who was speaking, the deep, masculine voice still sounded hauntingly familiar. She flinched and looked up, her heart nearly jumping out of her chest as her eyes focused on Alejandro. He was standing there holding a sign that said Fortune Robinson.

Instinct took over. She dropped her purse and ran into his waiting arms. He greeted her with the deepest, most possessive kiss and for a moment the entire world faded away. If she'd fallen asleep on the flight home, if she was dreaming this, she never wanted to wake up.

When they finally came up for air, he cupped her face with his hands. "I got your message."

"Which one? I left messages with both your dad

and Stefan, who is very nice, by the way. I met him in Miami."

Alejandro smiled. "I heard. I can't believe you went all the way to Miami. And I wasn't talking about either of those messages. I got the one that you left on my cell phone."

"How could you hear that message? I have your phone."

That reminded her that her purse and its contents were on the ground. When she stooped down to pick it up and gather her belongings, Alejandro bent down and helped her.

"Here it is, right here." She handed him his phone.

"I have a computer program that allows me to check my messages remotely. When I heard your voice and what you had to say, I knew I had to come to you right away. Olivia, I love you. How could we just walk away from each other?"

All she could do was shrug and shake her head.

"Let's never do that again. I almost grabbed a flight to see if I could meet you in Miami. But with the way we've been narrowly missing each other, I figured it would be best to be right here when you got home. Rachel gave me your flight information."

She hugged him again. "Alejandro, I'm so sorry for everything. I hope you can forgive me for pushing you away."

"Let me think about that for a moment." He turned over the sign and held it up. The other side read, "Olivia, will you marry me…for real?"

Her heart felt as if it would burst out of her chest. "You know how much I love champagne?"

"Yes," he said, his eyes locked with hers.

"You know I love it more than anything. But I love you more. I would give up champagne forever to have you."

"There's no need for you to give it up. Especially now."

"Why is that? Is it because you heard that there's another investor interested in joining you in the Hummingbird Ridge venture?"

His eyes flashed and she waited for him to ask if it was her father, but he didn't. So she offered the information. "It's me. I want to invest in you and Hummingbird Ridge and make it possible for you to be in Austin permanently."

"I would be here with or without Hummingbird Ridge. We will definitely talk about that later. But I want you to know I want to be with you, wherever you are. Obviously it isn't a good time to give up champagne. Because we'll need it to toast both of our partnerships—business and personal," he said. "But first, this time, I need to do this right, *querida*."

He pulled a familiar small red box out of his pocket and opened it. It was the fire opal ring she had put back in his briefcase.

He fell to one knee. "Olivia Fortune Robinson, will you do me the great honor of being my wife?"

"Yes! This time, I am not letting you get away."

As he slid the fire opal ring on her finger, a crowd of people broke into a rousing round of cheers and applause. It was her family—her sisters and brothers and their spouses. And his family—Orlando and Josephine and his sister and brothers. They were all there to see him propose.

He pulled her into his warm embrace, into that spot in his arms where she fit so perfectly. For the first time in her life, Olivia Fortune Robinson knew with her whole heart that love was real.

* * * * *

*Don't miss the next installment of
the Special Edition continuity*

*THE FORTUNES OF TEXAS:
THE SECRET FORTUNES*

*Quirky—but determined—blogger Ariana Lamonte
has spent months tracking down Fortunes near and
far. But when she crosses paths with rough and
ready cowboy Jayden Fortune from tiny Paseo,
Texas, will she discover a new branch of the family
tree—as well as love, small-town style?*

*Don't miss
WILD WEST FORTUNE
by*
NEW YORK TIMES *bestselling author
Allison Leigh*

*On sale June 2017, wherever
Harlequin books and ebooks are sold.*

Nell took a quick dash in the yard, then followed eagerly into the house. The dog was good at fitting in her business when she had the chance.

"Stay for a while," he asked Ashley. "I can offer you a soft drink if you'd like."

She held up her latte cup. "Still plenty here."

He rolled into the kitchen and up to the table, where he placed the box holding his extra meal. He didn't go into the living room much. Getting on and off the sofa was a pain, hardly worth the effort most of the time. He supposed he could hang a bar in there like he had over his bed so he could pull himself up and over, but he hadn't felt particularly motivated yet.

But then, almost before he knew what he was doing, he tugged on Ashley's hand until she slid into his lap.

"If I'm outta line, tell me," he said gruffly. "No social skills, like I said."

He watched one corner of her mouth curve upward. "I don't usually like to be manhandled. However, this time I think I'll make an exception. What brought this on?"

"You have any idea how long it's been since I had an attractive woman in my lap?" With those words he felt almost as if he had stripped his psyche bare. Had he gone over some new kind of cliff?

Don't miss
CONARD COUNTY HOMECOMING
by Rachel Lee, available June 2017 wherever
Harlequin® Special Edition books and ebooks are sold.

www.Harlequin.com

Celebrate 20 Years of

Love Inspired®

Inspirational Romance to Warm Your Heart and Soul

Whether you love heart-pounding suspense, historically rich stories or contemporary heartfelt romances, Love Inspired® Books has it all!

Sign up for the Love Inspired newsletter at **www.Loveinspired.com** and connect with us to find your next great read from the **Love Inspired, Love Inspired Suspense** and **Love Inspired Historical** series.

JUST CAN'T GET ENOUGH?

Join our social communities
and talk to us online.

You will have access to the latest
news on upcoming titles and special
promotions, but most importantly,
you can talk to other fans about your
favorite Harlequin reads.

Harlequin.com/Community

Facebook.com/HarlequinBooks

Twitter.com/HarlequinBooks

Pinterest.com/HarlequinBooks

Turn your love of reading into rewards you'll love with

Harlequin My Rewards

**Join for FREE today at
www.HarlequinMyRewards.com**

Earn **FREE BOOKS** of your choice.

Experience **EXCLUSIVE OFFERS** and contests.

Enjoy **BOOK RECOMMENDATIONS**
selected just for you.

PLUS! Sign up now
and get **500** points
right away!

Earn
FREE
REWARDS
Join
Today!
HarlequinMyRewards.com

MYR16R

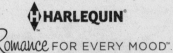